# JEOPARDY IN JULY

## A Jamie Quinn Mystery

By

Barbara Venkataraman

JEOPARDY IN JULY is a work of fiction. Names, characters, places, and incidents are either the product of the author's imagination or are used fictitiously. Any resemblance to actual persons, living or dead, events, or locales, is entirely coincidental.

Copyright © 2017 by Barbara Venkataraman

## Books by Barbara Venkataraman

*Death by Didgeridoo (A Jamie Quinn Cozy Mystery #1)*

*The Case of the Killer Divorce (A Jamie Quinn Cozy Mystery #2)*

*Peril in the Park (A Jamie Quinn Cozy Mystery #3)*

*Engaged in Danger (A Jamie Quinn Cozy Mystery #4)*

*Jeopardy in July (A Jamie Quinn Cozy Mystery #5)*

*I'm Not Talking About You, Of Course (Quirky Essays for Quirky People #1)*

*A Trip to the Hardware Store (Quirky Essays for Quirky People #2)*

*Teatime with Mrs. Grammar Person*

*If You'd Just Listened To Me In The First Place (Short Story)*

*The Fight for Magicallus (Children's Fantasy Story)*

*DEDICATED TO THE MEMORY OF*
*JESSIE SANDLER*

*YOUR BRIGHT SPIRIT LIVES ON*
*IN ALL OF US*

# Chapter One

With lights flashing, an ambulance pulled up to the front door of La Vida Boca before screeching to a stop. Prior to their arrival, the paramedics had disabled the siren out of deference to the three hundred elderly residents all of them in their eighties and nineties, with a few centenarians mixed in. It was wise not to startle them since only one stretcher fit in the back of the ambulance at a time. In truth, the old folks never got too excited about the ambulance anymore, but if a fire engine happened to show up, that got them out of their chairs in a hurry (relatively speaking) because who doesn't love a shiny red fire engine?

"Here comes the meat wagon again," Herb Lowenthal remarked, barely glancing up from his newspaper.

I was sitting in the opulent lobby of La Vida Boca, a five-star assisted living facility in Boca Raton, Florida and although I'd just met Herb I already had a pretty good handle on his world view.

"Welcome to God's waiting room," he added, laughing at his own joke. "Nobody in this place buys green bananas, if you know what I mean."

Not sure how to respond, I nodded and smiled. This was a first for me, hanging out at an old folks' home, and it was an eye-opener. Herb laid his crumpled newspaper down so he could study me over his smudged spectacles. Although his bushy eyebrows looked like two white caterpillars taking a nap, his inquisitive eyes missed nothing.

"What brings you here, Miss Jamie Quinn, is someone getting a divorce? Since when do lawyers make house calls?"

I gave him a friendly smile. "I can't tell you that, Herb. It's called attorney-client privilege. Just like on TV."

"Aha!" He pointed a knobby finger at me. "Someone *is* getting a divorce. Is it the Millers? Those two can never let go of anything. They're still arguing about whether Dewey defeated Truman. I wish I was kidding, oy vey."

I glanced at my watch. My clients were late, but I didn't

1

care, I would get paid no matter where I sat. "Before you go starting any rumors, Herb," I said, "you should know that I also prepare simple wills."

But I wasn't there to prepare a will; I wasn't wearing my 'lawyer hat' at all that day. I was there as a family mediator to mediate a divorce settlement--and no, it wasn't the Millers. I had mediated hundreds of cases over the years, but never one like this. After sixty years of marriage, Shirley and Clarence Petersen had suddenly decided to call it quits. As a divorce lawyer who had seen it all I shouldn't have been surprised, but as a woman who was recently 'engaged to be engaged' I was thrown off kilter. If Shirley and Clarence couldn't make it after six decades of trying, what hope was there for me and Kip? I pushed that thought away to focus on the work ahead.

My first order of business would be to establish whether both parties were competent. A basic tenet of contract law is that you can't enter into a contract if you're not in your right mind. Normally, each party would have an attorney who would've made that determination already but these two didn't want to pay for attorneys. That made it tricky for me. How could I tell? After all, a person with dementia could have lucid moments. As the saying goes, even a broken clock is right twice a day.

"Here they come with their next victim," Herb said matter-of-factly.

Two extremely buff male paramedics hustled by us pushing a wheeled stretcher between them. One of them held a portable oxygen mask over the patient's face, blocking it from view. I couldn't tell how serious the situation was but nobody seemed to be panicking. A few staff members followed them outside with paperwork and within five minutes the ambulance was on its way, siren turned back on.

I looked around the lobby wondering where my clients could be. Maybe they were already there waiting for me? I had no idea what they looked like. Before I could turn around, I had the wind knocked out of me and almost fell right out of my chair. A large chocolate Labradoodle had lunged out of nowhere and was now standing on his hind legs, front paws in my lap, trying

2

desperately to lick my face.

"Marley!" I exclaimed, scratching his head. "Aren't you a long way from home?"

# Chapter Two

Suddenly, everyone in the lobby sprang into action. Maybe *sprang* wasn't the right way to describe it, but two dozen old people were suddenly on the move, grabbing their walkers and canes, pulling dog treats out of their pockets, calling Marley's name and moving towards us at varying speeds. It might've been a little alarming but for the fact that they all looked so happy. I heard a familiar giggle behind me.

"Jessie Sandler!" I said. "What brings you all the way from Hollywood? If you and Marley were heading to the beach, you took a wrong turn, my friend."

She giggled again. "Hey, Jamie! How's it going? Believe it or not, we came here on purpose. We're here every week to do pet therapy with the residents and visit my Uncle Teddy. How about you? You're pretty far from Hollywood yourself. Looks like you got that blue paint out of your ears!"

The last time I'd seen Jessie had been a few weeks earlier at Precious Paws, her 1960s-rock 'n' roll-themed dog rescue where we had painted 'masterpieces' with the dogs while dancing to the Rolling Stones.

"That paint took a long time to wash off," I laughed, "but I had a blast! Did you sell the pictures?"

"Yes! I meant to tell you, I took your idea and made greeting cards and stationery. I also framed some of the prints and they're selling like wild. We made enough money to buy dog food for a year! Any time you're ready, we can do it again. My new dogs would love to paint--you know, express their creativity."

Only Jessie would think dogs had creativity to express. I was pretty sure my cat, Mr. Paws, wasn't stifling any artistic urges. He had no trouble expressing himself, especially when I left him alone overnight. Then, his royal highness would share his feelings by knocking a plant off the windowsill or a knickknack off a shelf-- exactly what Picasso must've done when he was pissed off.

"I'd love to!" I said. "Don't know when, but soon." I stood

up, leaving Marley to his admirers (which included my cheery new friend Herb) and pulled Jessie aside. "Do you know who Shirley and Clarence Petersen are? I was supposed to meet them here."

Standing next to Jessie, I marveled at how petite she was. Her energy and sparkle made her seem much taller than she actually was. Maybe because she was always smiling, I didn't pay attention to her other features, like her dark hair streaked with purple, or her pixie face with those sleepy eyes.

"I don't think I know Shirley," she said, "but Clarence is my Uncle Teddy's poker buddy." She scanned the room. "Nope, he's not here. Do you have their phone number?"

I shook my head. "I left it in my office, I'm such a space case."

Jessie walked me over to the front desk where a middle-aged black woman was busy answering the phones. After waiting patiently for the woman to notice her, Jessie interrupted.

"Hey, Glenda, quick question--have you seen the Petersens? They had an appointment with this lady and they're late."

Glenda gave Jessie a surprised look. "Didn't you see? Clarence Petersen was just taken away by ambulance. He collapsed on the shuffleboard court."

"How awful!" Jessie exclaimed.

I felt guilty that I hadn't been more sympathetic when I saw him carried out. It's like when you're stuck in traffic because of an accident and all you think about is how inconvenient it is for you. You forget that someone else is having a really terrible day. Maybe the stress of a looming divorce had made Clarence ill--although it seemed to me like he was the one pushing for it. Change was hard and I couldn't imagine doing it at the age of eighty-three.

"That's terrible news," I said. "I didn't know that was him they were carrying out. I hope he's okay." I looked around the lobby one more time and shrugged. "Well, I guess I'll get going, Jess, but I'm glad I got to see you and Marley."

"Do you really have to go?" she asked sweetly. "I could give you a tour."

Since I'd planned to spend several hours on the Petersen mediation (now officially canceled), I had nothing else going on.

5

And while I had zero interest in learning about the whirlwind excitement of assisted living, I did like hanging out with Jessie.
"Sure," I said. "Why not?"

# Chapter Three

"Next number, B-22. I'm warning you, people, someone better yell 'Bingo' soon. It's almost time for happy hour and there's a double martini calling my name."

Everyone in the Bingo hall laughed. The tiny white-haired woman with the big attitude was seated at a table in front facing the players. She continued calling out numbers and cracking jokes at a steady pace.

"That's Darlene," Jessie told me as we stood in the doorway. "She just turned a hundred and two, can you believe it?"

"She should do stand-up comedy," I said. "I'd have a drink with her."

Jessie nodded. "Me, too! But I'm not sure about the stand-up. I think she'd have to do sit-down."

I laughed. "That will be me someday, playing Bingo for nickels and counting the minutes 'til happy hour."

"Sounds like fun," Jessie said as she linked her arm in mine and led me away.

We peeked into the arts and crafts room where residents were busy making bracelets before moving on to the library with its overstuffed armchairs and extensive collection of thrillers, mysteries, and classics. A shelf dedicated to harlequin romances also held some racy bestsellers. A sign on the wall announced that Book Club met on Wednesdays. The thought of discussing *Fifty Shades of Grey* with women who reminded me of my grandmother sent shivers down my spine. You couldn't pay me to join that book club, not even for a million bucks. Well, maybe a million. Hell, I'd eat a cockroach for half that. Of course, a portion of my earnings would need to be set aside for psychotherapy and once the doctors invented a cool name for my syndrome--maybe Cockroach PTSD-- I'd be famous for the most disgusting reason imaginable. Go big or go home, I say.

"Next stop," Jessie said as we turned a corner, "you'll meet the coolest guys at La Vida Boca. They call themselves *The Card*

*Sharks.*"

I laughed. "So, they cheat at cards, but they let people know up front? Very considerate."

We passed a poster advertising movie night. The flick was *Pal Joey,* starring Frank Sinatra, Rita Hayworth and Kim Novak. It was easy to see why they had been such big stars; the women were beautiful and glamorous and Old Blue Eyes looked like he was loving life. Strolling through La Vida Boca was like traveling in a time machine. I wouldn't have been surprised to see people wearing 'I like Ike" buttons and humming Elvis Presley tunes--or to see Dr. Who hovering outside in the Tardis. How fun would that be?

"Tell me about pet therapy," I said as we continued walking through the long winding corridors. La Vida Boca was bigger than I'd thought. "How does it work?"

Jessie's face lit up. "Hooray! I get to talk about my favorite topic. Did you know that spending just fifteen minutes bonding with an animal sets off a chemical chain reaction in your brain that lowers your heart rate, blood pressure, and stress levels? Isn't that amazing? Pet therapy also helps people recover from illness and surgery and it can even help with memory. Have you ever heard of Sundowner's Syndrome?"

I shook my head. "It sounds like something bad happens when the sun goes down. Is it a fancy term for vampirism?"

Jessie punched me lightly in the arm. "Yeah, Jamie, all the old people turn into vampires. It's a deep, dark secret, so don't tell anyone."

I pretended to zip my lips and throw away the key. "Okay, now here's my deep, dark secret." I lowered my voice to a whisper. "When I was a kid, I was terrified of vampires. I used to sleep with the covers bunched around my neck so they couldn't get me. You can see that my strategy worked."

Jessie's eyes grew big in mock terror. "But, did it? I mean, maybe you *are* a vampire. You say you don't eat meat, but that could be one of your bloodthirsty tricks."

"I guess you'll have to stick around until after dark to find out," I said, baring my teeth.

Some things never change. I knew I'd be wrapping my

8

covers around my neck that night, just like the old days. It always worked--those vampires knew I had their number.

# Chapter Four

"Okay, I'll *bite*," I said. "What the heck is Sundowner's Syndrome?"

Jessie thought for a few seconds. "It's something that happens late in the day where people with dementia get confused and anxious, sometimes even aggressive. It's incredible how fast they can go from lucid to not knowing where they are or who you are."

"How does pet therapy help with that?" We were standing in the hallway outside the card room.

"Think about it--pets are soothing to be around, especially a trained dog like Marley. When someone is agitated and can't communicate, a friendly dog can calm him down. I mean, everyone can relate to a dog, even a baby, or an Alzheimer's patient."

"That's fascinating," I said, "but how many people can Marley work with at once?"

I pictured the lobby of La Vida Boca, the residents reading, napping, and socializing, a couple of hip grannies playing with their iPhones--until the sun goes down, at which point total chaos erupts and the scene transforms into a low-budget sci-fi movie or a cheesy horror film. Marley would need lots of back-up, maybe *all* the dogs from the shelter...

Jessie laughed. "It's not the zombie apocalypse, Jamie. A few people get confused and then Marley gives them what I call TLC."

"How is that different from regular TLC?"

"It's doggie love. A Tail wag, a Lick and a Cuddle."

"Got it," I said. "Can I borrow Marley when I need some TLC, or do I have to wait until I'm an old lady? I *am* pretty confused most of the time, if that helps."

"Okay, you're in. I'll put you on the schedule," Jessie said agreeably.

We entered the card room, a sunny space with a large window facing the tennis courts. The domino table was unoccupied as were the two Mahjong tables. In fact, the only people there were three elderly gentlemen and a spry-looking lady in her seventies wearing a dealer's hat and shuffling cards like a pro. She must have worked in Vegas or Atlantic City at some point, or maybe closer to home, like Seminole Hard Rock Casino. The four were seated around a green-felted table covered with poker chips.

"Jamie, this is my Great-Uncle Teddy," Jessie said fondly, resting her hand on the shoulder of a man who looked like the Monopoly guy. He had the same big white moustache, genial round face, and bald head. All he needed was a top hat.

"I don't know what's so great about him," joked the gray-haired man in plaid pants to Uncle Teddy's right. "He's a lousy poker player who hasn't won a game all week. I plan to spend his money on fast cars and loose women."

"Yeah, Harry, like you could handle either one," the woman teased as she dealt the cards.

"How far you gonna get on two dollars and fifty cents?" Uncle Teddy replied. "You can't even buy a *picture* of a fast car or loose woman with that kind of dough."

The black man with salt and pepper hair to Teddy's left laughed good-naturedly. "Enough trash talk, y'all," he said. "Time to play poker."

Uncle Teddy examined his cards like he was guarding state secrets before giving me a sly grin. "Why don't you and your friend sit down, Jess? Don't make the girl stand there. What's your name again, dear?"

"Jamie Quinn," I said, "nice to meet you."

"I'm Sylvia," said the dealer. "What brings you to La Vida Boca? Are you visiting someone?"

"I know you didn't come for the food," Harry said, making a face. "Stay away from the dining room, it's the worst. They think *salt* is a four-letter word, for God's sake."

"Salt *is* a four-letter word," said the man with the salt and pepper hair. "I'm Stanley, by the way."

I nodded and smiled. "Thanks for the advice. We should get going. Jessie is giving me a tour of the facility and we left Marley in the lobby with his adoring fans."

11

"When he's done, will you bring him in here?" Sylvia asked. "We're part of the 'Marley Fan Club' too, you know."

"Sure thing," Jessie said. "Hey, I heard about Clarence, what happened?"

Stanley looked serious. "He was complaining he didn't feel right and then boom! He just keeled over."

"It was probably indigestion," Harry said, trying to sound convincing. "The food here is awful, but it hasn't killed anyone. Not yet, anyway."

"I hope he's okay," I said.

"Me, too," Jessie said. "Now we're off to finish our tour." She gave her uncle a peck on the cheek. "Glad you're feeling better, Uncle Teddy, you look good."

He shrugged. "What can I say? I'm a good-looking guy."

# Chapter Five

"They are some interesting characters," I said.

Jessie laughed. "You're not kidding, and they say whatever's on their mind, too. I guess when you get old, you don't care what people think anymore."

"So there *is* a bright side," I said.

We walked through a set of glass doors to the pool where a water aerobics class was finishing up. Remarkably, not a single woman in the class had wet hair; all of them were still perfectly coiffed. I assumed the teacher had been given strict instructions about that. We kept walking and passed the shuffleboard court where Clarence Petersen had collapsed, then the tennis courts, a small putting green, and a picnic area with half a dozen tables. There was even a volleyball net strung over a sandy area. Considering that I couldn't hold my own in a game of volleyball, I wondered if the net was just for show, or whether I was in worse shape than an eighty-year old.

"I've been saving the best for last," Jessie said. We were standing by a wooden gate with an ornate iron handle which she unlatched with a bit of fanfare.

"Ta-da!"

The gate swung open to reveal a delightful garden that seemed to go on forever and I tried to take it all in. Mature fruit trees around the perimeter formed a natural border and included orange trees covered with tiny white blossoms, grapefruit trees, towering mango trees, some scattered guava and papaya trees, and a lone lychee nut tree covered with its trademark bumpy red fruit. Farther in, half a dozen pineapple plants had staked their claim alongside finger bananas that swayed in the breeze. To our right was a hothouse with exotic flowers and to our left a raised vegetable garden, each row neatly labeled with a tiny picture of the bounty to come. My favorite part was a large stand of bamboo in the center of the garden girded by a wooden shelf that held a dozen bonsaied plants. A path of dove gray pebbles wound gently away from the bamboo in concentric circles like ripples on a lake and teak benches offered a shady place to sit. The overall effect was balance and harmony and a Zen-like tranquility.

I told Jess I wanted to live there, meaning the garden, of course, not the old folks' home with its boring food and Sinatra reruns. I wasn't ready for *that* yet.

"I know what you mean," she said, "I love this place. Uncle Teddy thinks I come here to see him. Shh, don't tell him."

As we wandered around the garden, I thought about how much Kip would've enjoyed it. Then again, he would have been showing off the whole time, reciting the name of each plant, first in English and then in Latin--not his most endearing quality, I'm afraid. One time when we were in the Everglades together, we came upon a huge gator and I was freaking out, convinced we were goners. I started composing my farewell tweet to the world while Kip tried to distract me, droning on about mangroves and wetlands and ecosystems. He thinks if he ignores my crazy side, it will just go away. All I can say to that is *keep dreaming, babe.*

Jessie guided me toward the hothouse. "I want you to meet someone."

We paused in front of a sign posted at the entrance: *STOP. Are you wearing perfume? Are you allergic to bee stings? If so, please stay out of the hothouse for your own safety.*

Jessie gave me a questioning look and I shook my head. She pretended to sniff me so I sniffed her back and then we went inside.

Calling it a hothouse was an understatement--it was a sauna, a sauna with a couple of fans blowing hot air around. Granted, South Florida is always on the warm side, especially at midday in July, but it was *damn* hot in there. I planned to take a quick look around to be polite before escaping to the chilly embrace of the closest AC.

The sign inside the hothouse was more welcoming than the one outside. It read: "Flowers feed the soul" in colorful letters against a background of daisies. A strawberry blonde woman with her back to us was bending over a table filled with seedlings.

"Hey Jodi," Jessie said, "What are you growing this time?"

"See if you can guess." Jodi turned towards us with a playful expression. A friendly woman with intelligent hazel eyes, she looked to be in her mid-forties.

As we studied the plants, Jodi surveyed them with the pride of a mother duck counting her ducklings. I sensed something familiar about the plants once I considered the possibility that they might not be flowers.

"I have one of those growing in my refrigerator," I said, finally. "Which also proves I'm not a vampire," I said for Jessie's benefit.

"Oh, it's garlic," she said, "how fun!"

Jodi clapped me on the back. "You get an 'A' in horticulture," she said to me.

"And an 'F' in housekeeping," I laughed.

"It all depends on how low you set the bar," Jessie said. "Jodi, this is my friend, Jamie. Jamie, this is Jodi Martin, the activities director here."

"I knew you looked too young to be a resident," I said with a smile.

"Give me a few decades," she said. "I'll have to convince my husband first."

"Jodi is responsible for transforming this area into the Garden of Eden," Jessie gushed with a sweeping gesture that encompassed everything in sight.

"Now let's not get carried away," Jodi said, embarrassed. "I had lots of help. Which reminds me, have you met Eli yet? He's an amateur botanist and he's been teaching me so much. He used to live on the Ein Gedi Kibbutz where they have a world-famous garden. Come check out this weird plant he brought me."

As she led us to the far end of the hothouse, we passed lovely orchids in every color of the rainbow, some hanging from the ceiling, others in pots on the table, before we came to a table with the strangest plant I'd ever seen. Bright green leaves surrounded a hot pink vertical stalk which was shaped like a complicated TV antenna with horizontal stalks jutting out from it. At the end of each stalk was a white ball with a black dot in the middle that looked like an eyeball.

"What do you think?" Jodi asked.

15

Jessie shuddered. "It gives me the creeps! No way could I sleep with that thing in my room."

"What in the world is it?" I asked. When Kip was Parks Director, he had dragged me through every park in Broward County and I was sure I'd seen all the native species in Florida. "This has to be an invasive plant."

Jodi's face lit up. "I see you know a little something, but I'm afraid you're wrong. This beauty *is* a native and it's called White Baneberry, also known as Doll's Eyes. It actually grows in the wild."

I took out my phone and snapped a picture to send Kip. "It looks like a weird kind of Halloween candy."

Jodi laughed. "I don't know much about it, but I wouldn't eat it, it's probably poisonous. It's like what they say about mushrooms--all mushrooms are edible but some of them only once."

A happy bark signaled the arrival of Marley. He was with his buddy, Herb Lowenthal.

"Hey girls, it's almost lunchtime so I brought Marley back." Herb sounded winded.

"Thanks," Jessie said. "It's time for his walk anyway. I'll catch you next time, Jodi." She turned to me. "You coming?"

I watched with envy as Herb headed back to the place where cool breezes waft through vents, caressing the back of your neck and drying your sweaty forehead. With a parched throat and a body on the verge of mutiny, I heard myself say "All right, I guess."

# Chapter Six

Jesse and Marley were walking at a fast clip away from La Vida Boca.

"Where are we going?" I asked as I hustled to keep up with the dynamic duo.

"Oh, you know, chase squirrels, answer the call of nature--doggie stuff," Jessie answered.

My shoes weren't made for running and it was all I could do to keep from twisting my ankle on the uneven terrain. I had played hooky all morning and the emergency room seemed like a miserable way to spend the afternoon.

We had entered a densely wooded area filled with lush vegetation: looming oak trees, sabal palms, Surinam cherry bushes, ferns, vivid purple beautyberries, and my favorite, psychotria nervosa, also known as wild coffee. Its heavenly aroma made you understand why Adam and Eve decided to brew that first cup of Joe. I was just wishing I had an iced coffee when I spotted my least favorite plant, poison ivy. I pointed it out to Jessie.

She nodded. "Leaves of three, let it be."

I gave the ivy a wide berth as I watched Marley scamper through the woods, he was having a blast. Maybe scamper isn't the right word for a sixty pound Labradoodle, *bounding* was more like it.

I brushed a sticky cobweb off my arm in disgust. "Is this enchanted forest part of La Vida Boca?"

"Nah," Jessie said. "It's a nature preserve, part of the Palm Beach Parks Department. They have some awesome parks up here. You should see--"

She was interrupted by the urgent sound of Marley barking--something was wrong. Jesse took off running while I brought up the rear, tripping over my shoes. I was ten steps behind when all hell broke loose. Marley was growling and barking as a man cursed at him with gusto. By the time I got there, Jessie was hysterical and I could see why. Marley had cornered a man who had a knife in one hand and a machete in the other.

17

"Oh my God! Leave my dog alone--if you hurt him, I'll kill you! *Down*, Marley, I said get down now!"

Next thing I knew, Jessie had thrown herself on top of Marley. Terrified that the man would attack Jessie, I grabbed her waist from behind and tried to pull her away. Everyone was shouting and nobody was budging until finally the man yelled "I won't hurt your damn dog--*just get him off me!*"

The standoff ended peacefully when Jessie finally managed to yank Marley away. After the man left--which happened immediately--I realized my heart was pounding and my hands were shaking. Only then did it occur to me that I'd put myself in danger. It's funny but in a fight-or-flight situation I always assumed I'd run like hell. Turns out I'm an idiot. Good to know.

I wasn't the only one feeling the aftermath of our encounter, but where I was filled with nervous energy from our narrow escape, Jessie was furious.

"We have to call the police! That guy could be a serial killer stalking his next victim."

I shook my head. "We don't know that. Anyway, it's not illegal to carry a knife or a machete. Jeez, it's probably legal to carry a semi-automatic--we live in Florida, remember?"

Jessie knew I was right but she wasn't happy about it. She started racing towards La Vida Boca, a woman on a mission.

"What's the plan?" I asked, trying to keep up. Too bad I couldn't hitch a ride on Marley's back. Man, was I out of shape! I knew I shouldn't have erased that e-mail from my gym when they said they missed me. Of course they did, I was the one who made everyone else look good.

"I need to warn Jodi there's a maniac with lethal weapons lurking in the woods," Jessie replied.

"Hmmm," I said. "I'm not sure he's a maniac, but I'll give you the lurking part."

With the two of us at her heels, Jessie yanked open the garden gate and stormed into the greenhouse. Suddenly, she stopped short, gaping in horror, and I could see why. Jodi was standing near the bamboo, deep in conversation with someone we both recognized. Machete Man.

18

# Chapter Seven

Seeing him there, it was hard to believe this was the same person we'd thought looked so dangerous. In my mind, he had been taller, younger, and much more threatening than the man calmly talking to Jodi. It helped that he was now surrounded by beautiful flowers and that he wasn't brandishing any weapons. Context is everything. Upon closer scrutiny, I could see he was in his late sixties with a neatly-trimmed gray beard and precise mannerisms. He looked like a professor or the conductor of a symphony orchestra, exacting, decisive, in charge. Or maybe my imagination was just on overload. That was a definite possibility.

Jessie was having none of it. "Who do you think you are?" she demanded, wagging her finger practically in his face.

I didn't know her all that well but the Jessie I thought I knew was a giggly purple-haired savior of dogs who loved the Beatles, the Rolling Stones and tie-dye. This version of Jessie was a spit-fire, Jessie 2.0, and she wasn't taking crap from anyone.

Jodi looked shocked. "Jessie, what's going on here?"

"I'll tell you what's going on, *do not trust this man.* We caught him in the woods carrying an axe and a knife. Who does that? You don't scare me, Mister, so why don't you go intimidate somebody else!"

"That's not--you're making a--" Jodi interjected.

"--It's all right, Mrs. Martin, I can speak for myself," the man said touching her lightly on the arm. He was smooth, I'll give him that.

He turned to Jessie with a forced smile that never reached his eyes. "I apologize for the incident earlier, but I meant you no harm, I assure you. Your dog was being aggressive and blocking my path."

Jessie looked skeptical. "Who takes a nature walk carrying a knife and an axe?"

He stared her down, a pillar of composure and self-assurance. "I'm sorry if they offend you but those are my tools. I take cuttings of plants for grafting and cultivating."

Jessie's expression went from doubtful to smug. "I guess

you don't know it's against the law to remove plants from a nature preserve."

It was his turn to look superior. "And what you don't know is that this rule doesn't apply to me," he said disdainfully, then turned and walked away.

Jodi and Jessie were both shaking their heads, but for different reasons.

"That was a bit much, Jess, don't you think?" Jodi was wearing a pained expression.

"Why doesn't *he* have to follow the rules?" Jessie snapped. "What makes him so special?"

"He's a certified master naturalist, for one thing," Jodi explained.

"Well," Jessie said, not backing down, "he should wear a bell around his neck so he doesn't scare people to death. Seriously, all he needs is a mask and he'd look like Jason from *Friday the 13th*."

"I hate to tell you this," Jodi said, "but you're going to be seeing a lot more of him."

"Why?"

"Because he lives here. That's Eli, the botanist. He's the new resident."

Jessie scowled. I took that as my cue to take my leave before I passed out from heat stroke and needed my own ambulance with handsome paramedics.

"Hey Jess, I should go, I have a client coming in this afternoon. Thanks for the tour, it was fun. Or something." I laughed and Jessie did too. "Do me a favor?" I said. "Don't tell anyone I was here to see the Petersens, okay? Client confidentiality and all that."

"No problem," Jessie agreed. "Gossip is the only thing these folks enjoy more than Bingo."

"Thanks, and if I ever need an enforcer, I'm calling you. You're something else. But for now, try to play nice in the sandbox. Okay?"

"I'll try," she said making a face, "but it won't be easy. Come on, Marley, let's go see the Card Sharks."

20

# Chapter Eight

"Jamie, do you remember *La Nappe Mauve*?"

I was back at work and Jeff Rappaport, a former client, was sitting across from me at the conference table asking hard questions.

I stared at him blankly. "Sorry, but I don't. Isn't that French for *the purple tablecloth*?" I couldn't imagine why we were discussing purple tablecloths. My strange morning was now trending into afternoon.

"Maybe this will refresh your memory," he said, pushing a folded document into my hands.

I recognized it immediately. "This is the will I prepared for your father ten years ago. Does that mean...?"

He nodded, a flicker of sorrow in his eyes. "Dad passed away in January, he was ninety-two. He'd been living with us for the past few years. You know, when someone is a part of your life for so long it's hard to adjust when they're gone. Every day I wake up expecting him to be at the kitchen table reading the paper."

I knew what he meant; I still felt that way about my mother, especially since I was living in her house. "I'm sorry to hear that, Jeff, I liked Earl. He was a wonderful man with a great sense of humor. How is Tracy doing these days?"

Jeff perked up. "She's fantastic--the doctor gave her a clean bill of health and now she's training for a marathon. Can you believe it?" He rubbed his large belly and laughed. "I should probably take up running too."

Jeff's divorce from Tracy had been the most amicable I'd ever seen. Not only had they agreed on everything, but they were always joking around with each other. I couldn't understand why they were divorcing. A year later when Tracy needed surgery, Jeff had nursed her back to health. Next thing I knew, they were remarried.

"Sure, jogging is good for you," I said, "but so is a glass of wine. That's my kind of healthy living." I unfolded the will and glanced at it. "I'm afraid you've wasted a trip, Jeff, I can't help you with this. What you need is a probate attorney. I can give you some names if you like."

Jeff's round face flushed red and I remembered then how he could never hide his feelings. His face always gave it away.

"I *have* a probate attorney, Jamie. That's not why I'm here."

"Is there a problem with the will?" I couldn't imagine what it might be since I only prepared simple wills; the complicated ones were referred out.

"The will is fine, the problem is with the bequest. Please do me a favor and read it."

It's awkward to read with someone watching over your shoulder but, luckily, I read fast. Suddenly, it all came back to me. How could I have forgotten *La Nappe Mauve*? It was an original Chagall oil painting that was Earl's most prized possession. He told me it was the first thing he looked at in the morning and the last thing before bed. He was saving it for his children but wanted to enjoy it while he was still alive. I remembered seeing a photo of it and yes, there was a purple tablecloth, but it was such a small part of the painting it seemed hardly worth mentioning. The picture was a still life of a table with a fruit basket on the left and a tall vase of roses on the right--but I can't do it justice. *La Nappe Mauve* combined Impressionism and Modernism and was bursting with brilliant colors. It fooled you into thinking it was an Impressionist piece until you noticed the smiling horse peeking out from the roses. Then you saw a woman's face in the top left corner and a silhouette of a blue owl below that. It was a playful painting and I could see why Earl loved it.

I looked up at Jeff. "I remember now, it's an amazing piece. Did something happen to it?"

Jeff leaned forward, body taut as a spring. "Yes and no. Let me explain. My sister Cindy and I agreed to sell it at auction since there was no other way to divide the estate."

"It's not like you could cut the painting in half, right?" I laughed, but Jeff didn't look amused. "Sorry, bad joke, go on. Did you sell it?"

."No, the auction house rejected it. *They said it wasn't a Chagall*, just a very good copy, even though we had a certificate of authenticity!" As Jeff delivered this bombshell he tried to keep his anger in check.

I leaned back in my chair. "I don't understand. How did this happen?"

Jeff took a calming breath. "No idea. Here's the kicker, they told us the certificate of authenticity was genuine, but the painting wasn't."

I took a sip of water and wondered what advice to offer. What did Jeff expect from me? I mean, I'm not a magician.

"That's terrible news," I sympathized. "Did you go to the police? Or the FBI?"

He shook his head, embarrassed. "What would I say, that I think my dad got swindled forty years ago?"

"True." I waited a beat before asking the obvious. "So, why come to me?"

Jeff shrugged. "My sister is in meltdown and refuses to deal with this. She spent her inheritance before she got it and now she's in debt up to her eyeballs. The probate attorney is useless and the only thing the auction house could tell me is that the real painting hasn't been sold--at least not through legitimate channels--in the last forty years. I was hoping maybe you took some notes when you prepared my dad's will, or that you might remember something he told you. It was a long shot, but I didn't know where else to turn."

I can't stand it when people come to my office to tell me their tale of woe expecting me to fix it. I hate it because I can't say no. I don't know why that is--either I'm a classic textbook 'rescuer' or a glutton for punishment. My friend Grace would say I'm both.

When I didn't send him on his way, Jeff looked encouraged. "You always have good ideas, Jamie. What do you think I should do?"

I didn't want to get his hopes up. "Beats me," I said. "Unfortunately, I don't keep files more than seven years, so I wouldn't have any notes and I don't remember anything except what I already told you. If you can't find out who sold the painting to your dad, maybe you can discover who owned it before. Was it insured?"

"I thought so--my dad actually told me it was insured--but I can't find the policy anywhere and I've gone through his papers a dozen times. Maybe I should hire a private investigator..."

I nodded in agreement, a big smile on my face. "I know just the guy--he's very good and works for cheap. He doesn't have an office, but you can usually find him at *The Big Easy* on Harrison Street."

# Chapter Nine

Jeff read the business card I handed him and chuckled. "The guy's name is *Marmaduke*? Like the dog in the comic strip?"

"Yeah, I wouldn't bring that up," I said, "sore subject. Just call him Duke." I paused. "Do you want me to give him a heads-up about your situation? I owe him a call anyway." *What was wrong with me? Why did I have to be so damn helpful? It was borderline pathological...*

Jeff nodded gratefully. "That would be terrific, Jamie. I've been so upset about this but Tracy said you'd know what to do. That woman is always right, it's uncanny."

"Must be why you married her," I teased.

"Twice!" He laughed. "After the first time, I learned my lesson. She's stuck with me now."

"Celebrating two anniversaries a year must get expensive."

"You got that right," he said, "but she's worth it."

After I saw Jeff out, I sat down at my desk to listen to messages and read e-mail. Nothing urgent or complicated jumped out at me so I went on auto-pilot as I mulled over Jeff's problem. Even if Duke discovered who sold the fake Chagall to Earl (as unlikely as that was), what could Jeff do about it? File a law suit? Press charges? The seller was either a conman or he'd been duped himself; in any case, he was probably dead by now, it had been so long. And locating the insurance policy wouldn't do much good. No way in hell an insurer would pay a claim for a counterfeit painting. Jeff would be better off setting it on fire. Just kidding--an upstanding attorney like me would never suggest anything as illegal as that. Last time I checked, committing arson and insurance fraud weren't on my bucket list.

My mind wandered to my favorite subject, my almost-fiancé Kip. After three months in Australia saving the Northern Hairy-Nosed Wombat, he was finally coming home--about time, too. Nothing much had happened in his absence, I only took on the biggest case of my career, had a falling-out with my best friend Grace, was blackmailed with pictures of Duke kissing me, threatened with disbarment, helped solve three murders and almost got whacked by the Russian mob. And I thought I'd be bored.

As if that weren't exciting enough, I'd also received a marriage proposal (from Kip, of course), but when he tried to pop the question over Skype (every girl's dream, right?), I had to call a time-out. Face to face means *in person* in my book, so our happy reunion would be the official kick-off to our happy union. I told Kip I would resist hunting for the engagement ring he'd hidden somewhere in my house but if I happened upon something shiny it wouldn't be my fault, right? Okay, I'll admit it, I looked for it, but Kip hid it too well. At least I'd kept my promise not to move while he was away--as if that would happen. Anyone who knows me knows I don't like to stir things up. In my world, an object at rest tends to stay at rest and if you look up inertia in the dictionary, you'll see my picture. Thinking about my erstwhile high-school beau and almost-fiancé was too much for me. I pulled out my phone and sent him a text.

*Hey K, miss you! Hurry home. Love, your secret admirer*

To my surprise, he answered right away. Usually the time difference caused a delay.

*Hmmm, which secret admirer is this? Is it the sexy one?*

*You're lucky you guessed right,* I texted.

*It's the luck of the Irish, Babe.*

*Shame you're not Irish,* I pointed out. *By the way, did you lose something shiny in my house?*

*Tell me you didn't--did you??*

*Nah, I'm just messing with you,* I texted. *Can't wait to see you in a week!*

*Can't wait to see you either, Jamie, but I'm afraid there's been a change of plans.*

*Always joking around, that's why I love you.*

*I wish I were joking,* he messaged, *but there's something I have to do first.*

*Have to, or want to? Haven't you saved enough wombats already?* I didn't need emojis to get my point across, I was ticked off.

*Don't be mad and it's not wombats, it's tree snakes.*

*Dammit, Kip! Why do you need to save tree snakes?*

26

*I'm not saving them, I'm eradicating them. They're a menace.*

*So how many months will this project take?* I was ready to bang my head on the desk in frustration.

*All it takes is one long plane ride over Guam, two thousand dead mice in parachutes and a whole lot of Tylenol.*

*And?* I texted back.

*Maybe another month.*

# Chapter Ten

*Why would you agree to do that? When were you going to tell me?* I was texting so fast the words were a jumble but autocorrect had my back.

A long minute passed before Kip responded. *I was going to call you tonight, Babe, I swear. I just can't pass it up, when will I have a chance like this again?*

I thought my head was going to explode. *That's what you said about the wombats! Do what you want, Kip. I can't compete with tree snakes and dead mice.*

*Jamie, please try to understand. Can we talk about this later over Skype?*

*There's nothing to talk about. I have to go.*

I turned off my cell and shoved it in a desk drawer and then slammed the drawer for good measure. Not the most mature way to handle things, I know, but it was the best I could do. My world was collapsing and I felt like I was about to throw up. Thunderstruck, blindsided, ambushed--three words I'd never understood before that moment. This kind of thing happened to other people, not me. Problem-solving, helpful to a fault, clueless Jamie Quinn, the woman with all the answers. How stupid was I to think that Kip would come home and live an ordinary life after going to Australia? He wanted adventure, he craved it, and I was clearly holding him back. Of course I would wait another month if I had to, that wasn't the issue, but how could I spend my life with a man who dreamt of saving the world only to wake up every day in mind-numbing suburbia? Days spent cleaning out the gutters and fixing the fence, rotating tires and changing the oil, punching a clock and counting the days to retirement--that wasn't Kip. And chasing around the globe saving endangered animals wasn't me. I happened to enjoy mind-numbing suburbia. A good book, a steaming cup of Earl Grey, a purring cat on my lap, and rain pattering on the window was my idea of a perfect Sunday afternoon--the kind of afternoon I'd hoped to spend with Kip. Like I said, I'm an idiot.

I wanted to crawl under my desk and never come out, but it was after five and the office was closing. My being miserable was no reason to give the cleaning crew a heart attack. Reluctantly, I retrieved my phone from the drawer and threw it in my purse. In a haze, I made it to the parking lot and into my Mini Cooper where I picked up my keys but didn't start the car. Instead, I laid my throbbing head on the warm steering wheel and sat there for several minutes in the empty lot, incapable of moving. There was no point to anything. What was my plan now? Adopt a hundred cats and become a crazy cat lady? Right--I could barely handle one cat. Who was I kidding, nothing could replace Kip. Not cats or rain or hot tea or all the books in the world, all I wanted was him. I didn't care if he came with an entire zoo, like Dr. Doolittle, and we had to live in Puddleby-on-the-Marsh, wherever that was. If only we *could* live inside a novel, everything would be perfect. Elizabeth Bennet and Mr. Darcy together forever.

Being a drama queen was so much easier than I'd thought. All those years, I'd assumed my clients had to work at it but all you had to do was take one mundane life, turn it upside down and shake vigorously. But, unlike my client who had chained herself to the flagpole in front of the courthouse or the one who smashed her husband's prize guitar in his workplace lobby, I wasn't into performance art. I was more brooding, angsty. When my mother had succumbed to cancer four years ago, I was in a rut and for six months I hardly left the house. But that wasn't me anymore. Since then, I'd been through so much and faked it so often I'd convinced myself I had my act together. Like clapping for Tinkerbell, believing in something can make it real--or real enough, anyway. My real fear was that Kip was Peter Pan and he would never grow up while I was Wendy, unimaginative and unadventurous--in a word, boring. It seemed like Kip had finally figured that out; too bad it wasn't before he'd bought me an engagement ring. I wish we could have been more like my dad and his wife, Ana Maria, who were making their marriage work against all odds despite the fact that she was in Florida and he was stuck in Nicaragua. When my dad found a job that sent him on the road, I'd had to postpone my trip to finally meet him in person. Now, after Kip's bombshell, my calendar was suddenly wide open. I could book that flight…

I was still sitting in the parking lot lost in thought when someone knocked on my window and scared the daylights out of me.

# Chapter Eleven

Jolted from my reverie, I quickly started the car and shifted into reverse before risking a peek through the window. It wasn't a bad neighborhood or anything but you never know. What I saw was a white guy in dark sunglasses and a black baseball cap turned backwards. He had scraggly facial hair and a thick silver chain hanging halfway down his wife beater t-shirt. Baggy jeans and expensive sneakers completed the ensemble, but it was the fake arm tattoos that got me. After the day I'd had, I found the whole thing hysterically funny.

I turned off the car and opened the window in a fit of giggles. "Oh my God, Duke, what are you wearing? You look ridiculous! Did you lose a bet or something? Wait, don't move!" I pulled my phone out of my purse and snapped his picture. "Oh, this is even better than your pirate costume from the Ren Fest--and that was classic."

Duke took off his sunglasses and struck a pose, flexing his biceps and adjusting his cap. "For your information, Ms. Esquire, I am undercover. A good P.I. has to blend into the crowd, you know, stalking his prey like a ninja."

That set me off into peals of laughter. "You call that blending in? You look like an Eminem wannabe. Let's hear you rap about how the man is keeping you down. Come on, Broussard, blend!

With a sly look on his face, Duke said "Watch this" and laid down some Eminem right there in the parking lot. He transformed himself into a rapper, and a robot--and he was really good, too.

*I'm beginning to feel like a Rap God, Rap God*
*All my people from the front to the back nod, back nod*
*Now who thinks their arms are long enough to slap box, slap box?*
*They said I rap like a robot, so call me rap-bot.*

When he finished, he dropped an invisible mike while I clapped and whistled my approval.

"You're a man of many talents, Duke!"

31

He leered. "That's what all the girls say, Darlin'."

I rolled my eyes. "Aw, I walked right into that. When will I learn?"

He laughed, showing off his gleaming teeth, and then gave me a quizzical look.    "When I saw your car, I decided to stop by, found you hugging the steering wheel. What's the deal, Jamie? You okay?"

I shrugged, embarrassed. "Rough day, just needed a break. It's all good."

I knew he didn't believe me and he knew I wouldn't tell him the truth, so he let it go, but he couldn't resist being a smartass.

He leaned into my open window, mischief in his eyes. "If Lover Boy isn't treatin' you right," he said in his Louisiana drawl, "I could give him some advice."

I snorted. "*You're* going to give Kip advice? In the time that I've known you, how many women have slapped you, dumped you, or plastered your face on a billboard? Shall I name them? I'm keeping a list."

Duke laughed. "That billboard was somethin', wasn't it? I sure met my match in Candy Broussard. We had some hellacious arguments, but I still miss that woman."

"Yeah," I said, "real good times." I started my car again. "Well, I don't want to keep you from being a ninja or whatever. I almost forgot, a guy named Jeff Rappaport wants to hire you. I gave him your number."

"Hire, as in pay me money? Yee haw! What's the story?"

I smiled coyly. "Oh, just the usual--art forgery, scams on senior citizens, missing insurance policies, desperate beneficiaries. Nothing you can't handle." I shifted into reverse. "You might want to change your outfit before you meet him, though. Not sure Jeff's into rap." I laughed. "How much are you getting for this gig, anyway?"

"It's a favor."

I nodded. "Of course it is. For one of your barfly friends, I suppose. Maybe he'll buy you a drink."

Duke gave me a salacious wink. "I'm sure she will."

32

## Chapter Twelve

The drive home was short and uneventful in that I wasn't accosted by any more rappers, fake or otherwise. Because my office was just a mile from my house on Polk Street, I made it home in ten minutes flat. At rush hour, it would've been a whopping fifteen. Downtown Hollywood is so small that if you blink you'll miss it, which is why lawyers like me take cases in neighboring cities. It's not that we want to, but it helps us afford the luxuries in life, like rent and office supplies.

I emptied my mailbox straight into the recycle bin and then opened the door to receive my scolding from Mr. Paws. *How dare I come home late! Didn't I know he was hungry? This wouldn't have happened if my mother were around.* More than once I'd considered buying an automatic feeder to dispense with all the drama, but I knew it wouldn't work. His Highness would only eat smelly canned food served in his favorite bowl by his favorite servant--me. He was twelve pounds of fun and had earned his nickname of Mr. Pain in the Ass. Clearly, I could never be a crazy cat lady, which was a relief, but also narrowed my options.

If you're wondering whether I'd heard from Kip, I was wondering that, too, but I refused to look at my cell to find out. With the ringer turned off, my phone was like Schrodinger's hypothetical cat, neither dead nor alive until someone bothered to check it. Impulsive by nature, I normally didn't exercise much self-restraint, but I knew that no good would come from looking at my phone. There was nothing Kip could say that would undo what he'd done and what that meant for the future of our relationship. The bottom line was he didn't want to come home. The fact that I'd been waiting for him for months, dying to see him, didn't seem to matter. If he offered to give up the trip to Guam, I'd know it was only to appease me, not because he wanted to. If he *didn't* offer, that would speak volumes as well. It was a lose/lose scenario. Doing nothing wasn't really a decision, it was just me burying my head in the sand.

After a glass of Merlot, some warmed up leftovers and a rerun of Castle, I passed out on the couch where I dreamt I was being chased by snakes as dead mice gracefully parachuted onto my head like tiny ballerinas. It was a fitting end to my bizarre day and I had Kip to thank for it.

Eventually, the noise of the television roused me from my stupor and I stumbled to my room knowing that sleep time was over. As usual, I laid in bed for hours, too tired to get up, too wired to fall asleep. Staring wide-eyed at the ceiling, it occurred to me that I could paint something up there, maybe sheep to count or a "Where's Waldo" picture to help me pass the time. Kind of like Michelangelo and the Sistine Chapel, but without the divine inspiration.

On the plus side, a self-employed insomniac can sleep in without fear of being fired. Although I couldn't avoid early-morning hearings altogether, I could plan for them by setting a cascade of alarms at fifteen minute intervals. If all hell didn't break loose in the morning, I'd know it was safe to keep sleeping. My backup contingency was, of course, Mr. Paws, who had his own schedule to keep. By eight-thirty, if I wasn't awake, he'd start meowing. If that didn't work, he'd walk across my stomach a few times and if that failed he'd start batting me in the face. I wasn't a fan of his methods but I had to admire his work ethic.

My rough night rolled into a triple-espresso morning and if I wanted to avoid a migraine there was no time to waste. First step, insert nose in coffee canister and inhale deeply to kick-start brain. Next step, scoop, tamp, steam and repeat until iced latte splashed across my excited palate and caffeine molecules danced a conga line through my bloodstream. I noticed that the older I got, the more poetic I could wax about coffee.

Ready to officially start my day, I dressed like a lawyer and turned my phone on like a grown-up. I had numerous messages and e-mails and one voicemail, which wasn't from Kip. I pushed play.

"Hey Jamie, it's Jess. Sad news, Clarence Petersen didn't make it. I thought you'd want to know. Uncle Teddy is taking it hard. Call me when you can."

While I never had the chance to meet Clarence or Shirley,

part of me was relieved that their sixty year marriage didn't end in divorce; that would've been awful. Yes, I know, I should have picked a different career. It turns out being a divorce lawyer wasn't really my thing.

# Chapter Thirteen

When I showed up at work on Tuesday, the waiting room was packed and our receptionist had her hands full signing people in. Thankfully, nobody was there to see me; they were all there for Nelda. I shared space with a cheerful worker's comp attorney named Nelda Santos who couldn't keep up with the pool of potential clients claiming to have been injured on the job. With the collection of crutches, neck braces, and bandages on display that morning, the waiting room looked like a scene from *ER* or *Grey's Anatomy*, or any disaster movie ever made. Anyone seeing that would think Hollywood, Florida was a dangerous place to work indeed. It was a wonder nobody had called OSHA yet.

I waited until I was at my desk, warm sunlight streaming through the window, to learn what news, if any, there was from Kip. I discovered that during the night he'd sent me a dozen texts of increasing length and urgency all sprinkled with emojis--worried faces, hearts, a crying cat, a storm cloud, a rotary phone, and, for some reason, 4th of July fireworks. Here's the gist of it.

*Babe?*

*Babe? You there?*

*Jamie, can we talk about this?*

*It's been 4 hours, can you text me back please? I'd settle for #$@&%\*! or a pissed-off emoji.*

*Okay, I get it, you're giving me the silent treatment, but now I'm worried. I think it's time for reinforcements...You asked for it--I'm calling in the troops.*

I had to laugh. Kip assumed I was giving him the silent treatment--which I guess I was--but I wasn't doing it to punish him; I was trying not to face some hard truths about our relationship. One thing I'd learned in my years as a lawyer, the best tool in a negotiation is silence. I'd won more for my clients by sitting back and doing nothing, as the other side panicked and wound up sweetening the deal. Who says lawyers get paid by the word? It's the results that matter, baby. And I'm good at doing nothing; in fact, it's

36

my specialty.

I soon learned what Kip meant by reinforcements. The first call came from Aunt Peg inviting me to lunch to celebrate her summer break from teaching. She was dying to catch up with me, *she said*, she hadn't seen me in so long she forgot what I looked like, *she said*. But when she asked if I'd heard from Kip, I knew what the call was really about. I told her I had to run but promised we'd get together soon.

My policy is that when I'm at work I have to do some work so I shuffled through the files on my desk and found one that required attention. The Schwartzes had a hearing coming up and I needed to research a few issues. No sooner had I signed into my favorite legal research site (the free one), than I was interrupted by a text from my cousin Adam inviting me to go to the bark park with him and his three dogs, Angus, Bono, and Beast, after work. It sounded like fun and I was about to say yes when I realized I couldn't since I'd just blown off his mother not five minutes earlier and I didn't want to hurt Aunt Peg's feelings. Then I realized she had probably put him up to it in the first place. *Duh, Jamie.*

I returned to my research and came up with a few cases to support my position. Unfortunately, they weren't from our district, so not as good as I'd hoped. The only thing better than a Fourth District opinion on my side would've been a Florida Supreme Court case--and good luck finding that. As they taught us in law school, if you have the facts on your side, hammer the facts; if you have the law on your side, hammer the law. If you have neither the facts nor the law, hammer the table.

My next interruption came from Ana Maria, my dad's wife. When I'd found my long-lost dad, I'd also gained a wonderful step-mother. There wasn't a nicer lady on the planet than Ana Maria. Kindness oozed from her pores and concern for her fellow man was her mantra. She was the type of person you'd expect to run a homeless shelter, which is what she did. When Ana Maria called, she said that she'd spoken with my dad, that his job was going well and that he missed us. I was sure he missed her more but didn't say so. Why state the obvious? Ana Maria wanted everyone to feel loved, that was her way. When she finally asked about Kip, it seemed like an afterthought and I gave her the benefit of the doubt because Ana Maria was incapable of trickery or nefarious intent.

I finished with the Schwartz file having done the best I could and moved on to my next problem which was ridiculous, to say the least. The Palmers were arguing about bunk beds for their twins. Mom wanted them but Dad was vehemently opposed and had extensive documentation to prove they were deathtraps. Naturally, I represented Doomsday Dad--what a party he was. I didn't have kids, but I knew you couldn't protect them from everything or swaddle them in bubble wrap. It made them neurotic or turned them into Evel Knievel. I was thinking about *The Flying Wallendas,* how even after several family members were killed on the high wire, they still kept courting death when I was interrupted by a text from Duke asking how I was doing. I couldn't accuse him of being on Kip's payroll after he'd seen me moping in my car, so I texted back that I was fine. He agreed that I *was* fine, a fine specimen of womankind. That Duke, you gotta love him.

I'd almost finished drafting my dramatic motion about the dangers of bunk beds when my cell rang. It was Grace, who never called me during work hours barring an emergency.

I answered with, "Et tu, Brute"?

"If I'm Brutus, that makes you Caesar, and I'm not sure I like where this is going. Just what are you implying, young lady?"

"I'm not implying anything, I'm stating it outright. You're a traitor. I know Kip asked you to check on me."

"Well," she said, "I'm not gonna lie, but you shouldn't be so hard on him. He was ready to hop on a plane and come see for himself."

"Oh, sure he was!" I huffed, feeling the effect of three espressos and no sleep pushing me into crazy land. "Let's see, should I go home to my loving girlfriend and propose, or should I go to Guam and kill tree snakes? Who's the lucky winner, Johnny? It's tree snakes!"

Grace laughed. "I know you're mad, but listen to me. Having dated my fair share of losers, I think Kip is worth hanging onto, don't you? Just talk to him--after you cool off, of course, and you'll work it out. Okay?"

I took a breath. "I'll think about it. Right after I figure out where your loyalties lie."

"I'm on your side, Jamie, come hell or high water. You know I'd even bail you out of jail."

"A real friend would be in the cell with me," I said.

"Don't be silly. Then who would file the writ of habeas corpus?"

I smiled. "You really are on my side, Gracie."

# Chapter Fourteen

"Do I have to wind up in jail to see you?" I asked, "Because that could take a while. How about instead we hit a happy hour on Friday and I'll tell you my tale of woe."

"That doesn't sound happy at all," Grace laughed. "I'd love to, but I promised Nick I'd go to a meet and greet with him at the Riverside Hotel. You know, the life of a politician."

"Hmmm…how does that work then?" I asked. "Are you a politician if you're just running for office or do you have to actually *hold* office?"

"For your information, smartass, candidates for office are also considered politicians. You and Nick love to rag on each other; don't you? You're like a brother and sister fighting for mom's attention."

"I hope that doesn't mean you're our mom! There's a Greek tragedy waiting to happen." I couldn't help myself. Nick Dimitropoulos brought out the snark in me even when he wasn't in the room. "Sorry, Gracie, I couldn't resist. You set that up so perfectly."

She sighed. "I did, didn't I? Well, as much as I enjoy our little chats where you pick on my boyfriend, I should get back to work. You wouldn't understand the scourge of billable hours and partners breathing down your neck."

I shuddered. "And I hope I never do! Oh yeah, one more thing. Did you talk to your friend Greg at the State Department about my dad's visa? What's going on with that?"

Grace hemmed and hawed and promised to get back to me, but she was acting kind of strange. Not like she'd forgotten, more like she was hiding something. I couldn't quite put my finger on it but decided to let it slide. I couldn't handle any more bad news.

After eating leftover pizza from the breakroom fridge, I broke down and texted Kip. *Hey Babe, I'm ok, I just had my phone turned off. Thanks for sending out the troops, a/k/a everyone I ever met. When the mailman checks on me later, I'll give him your regards, lol. We do need to talk*

40

*about stuff, but I'm not ready yet. Maybe in a couple of days? xoxo*

Kip may have been a wombat-saving, adventure-seeking tree hugger, but I still loved him, even though he drove me nuts.

For the rest of the afternoon, I finished working on some odds and ends and then tidied up my desk because I had a consult scheduled for the end of the day. I was so tired I didn't think I could find the energy to land a new client and wasn't sure I even wanted to.

At four o'clock, a woman in her early thirties whirled into my office in a cloud of expensive perfume, right on time. She looked like a Boca socialite to me and I knew from experience that sleek hair like hers with all its highlights and lowlights cost about two hundred dollars at the salon. Yet, for all her glam accessories, Tory reminded me most of a skittish cat. I smiled reassuringly and offered her a seat.

"Why don't you tell me what's going on, Tory, and I'll see if I can help you."

Her bottom lip quivered and I instinctively reached for the box of tissues.

"I'm...I'm scared of my husband...he's tried to kill me-- twice!" she sobbed.

No way in hell was I taking this case; a violent husband was persona non grata in my book. I would do my best to steer her in the right direction, give her a referral, maybe some tea and sympathy, and send her off.

"Are you looking for a restraining order?" I asked. "Or a divorce as well?"

"Everything, all of it! I want to sue him for personal injury and emotional damage, too. You have no idea what he's put me through."

Tory was angry now, but at least she had stopped crying. She was tapping her long manicured nails on the arm of the chair which set my teeth on edge. The sooner she left the better. It was like interviewing someone for a job when you knew after the first thirty seconds that you weren't going to hire them.

"Did you file any police reports?" I asked.

She shook her head.

41

"Okay, have you requested a restraining order before?"

Tory shook her head again.

"Have you ever gone to a shelter or received counseling as a victim of domestic abuse?"

"No, I haven't," she said, looking like she was about to start crying again.

"Do you have any photographs of bruises or anything like that?" I asked.

"No, I don't," she answered.

"Has he threatened you with a gun or a knife?"

She shook her head. "Topher doesn't own a gun."

*Topher? Like rhymes with gopher? What kind of name was that?*

"Okay, has *Topher* hit you with his fists or any objects?"

"That's not how it is, you don't understand!" She slapped the arms of the chair in frustration.

I sighed. "I'm trying to understand, Tory. You said Topher has tried to kill you twice. Can you tell me what happened?"

"When he gets angry, he says he's going to kill me and make it look like an accident."

I was losing patience. "Can you be more specific? I'm imagining all kinds of things, like him throwing the toaster into the bathtub..."

"Not that kind of accident. He chases me around the house with a--"

"--With a what, Tory?"

"With a spoonful of peanut butter! I'm allergic to peanuts."

# Chapter Fifteen

I know that a peanut allergy is a serious thing, so why did I feel like laughing? Imagining Topher chasing Tory around the house wielding a spoonful of peanut butter was too ridiculous, I couldn't take it. Feigning a coughing fit, I dashed out of the room for some water. Once in the breakroom, I tried to get a grip but the more I tried not to laugh the worse it got. Stress and lack of sleep were fueling my fit of giggles and I couldn't stop. Just then, Nelda Santos came looking for her afternoon coffee and wanted in on the joke. Gasping, I told her the story in the hope of regaining my composure. Bad idea.

"Oh, dios mio!" Nelda squealed. "That's hilarious!" Then she started laughing, too. And I thought yawning was contagious.

"Okay, okay," I said, slapping my face a few times, "I *have* to go back in there." I didn't dare look at Nelda for fear of cracking up again.

As I walked towards my office, I suddenly realized I felt much better. There's nothing like a good laugh or a good cry to clear your head, although only one of them is enjoyable.

Tory was awaiting my return looking skittish once more and I felt bad for her. I sat down and gave her the good news first. To qualify for an initial restraining order all she had to do was testify under oath that Topher had threatened her with bodily harm and that she was afraid of him. Suing him for personal injury was more complicated, however, because she would have to prove damages, which in her case were psychological. I suggested that she start counseling so she could obtain a diagnosis, a prognosis, and medication, if necessary. Then I gave her referrals for three attorneys who handled restraining orders.

As I saw her out I gave her more advice. "You're in a toxic relationship, Tory, and you need to leave. Vacating the home won't jeopardize your interest in it, so you might want to go stay with a friend or relative for a while. Can you do that?"

She gave me a sad smile. "My parents fight non-stop and

my sister is in the middle of a divorce herself. Maybe my cousin will let me stay in her spare room..."

I wished her luck and then started to close down my office for the night. Money hadn't brought Tory happiness, I thought, but it had to make her life easier. As for me, I was having an existential crisis of my own and it wasn't about Kip. Being a family attorney had become a major drag and I wanted out. All that time and money for law school wasn't so I could spend my time dividing DVD collections and arguing about nonsense. It's not what I signed up for--but what did I sign up for? I had no idea, but I knew what my mother would've said. She'd say, Jamie, sit down and make a list. Feeling a new sense of urgency, I switched the lights back on, grabbed a legal pad from my desk and started scribbling notes.

My first priority was to stay self-employed, of course, but even that was negotiable in the short term. To narrow the options, I eliminated those areas of practice I found distasteful or difficult. Personal injury and medical malpractice were out because I didn't have the support staff or the money to cover the costs. Worker's comp didn't sound like fun, but working for Nelda did, so I put that in the *maybe* column. I didn't mind research and writing, but doing it every day would be torture, so appellate work was out. Ditto for contract law. For estate planning, I'd have to go back to school (horrors!) for a masters in tax. Considering I'd once spent two hours trying to balance my checkbook only to realize I'd subtracted the date by mistake, tax law wasn't for me. Of course, immigration law was near and dear to my heart because of my dad's situation, but I didn't speak Spanish, Creole or Portuguese. Corporate work was complicated and nasty and I didn't want to be anyone's hired gun, so that was out too. I didn't like insurance defense because denying claims to hapless people would keep me up at night and how could I possibly stand to sleep any less?

My problem was I wanted to be the good guy wearing the white hat at all times and that was impossible. I thought about doing bankruptcy work but it sounded too depressing, same for elder law. Suddenly, it came to me--probate! Probate was straightforward and interesting, the paperwork was balanced out by client contact and the fees were paid by the estate, so no billable hours. As they say, a will is a *dead giveaway*, ha ha. Energized, I logged onto the Florida Bar website and downloaded some continuing ed classes on probate law. All I had to do now was send some good vibes into the universe and hope they found their way back to me.

Then the phone rang...

# Chapter Sixteen

Startled, I knocked my cell off the desk onto the floor and scrambled to grab it before it stopped ringing. After breaking several phones, I'd finally gotten smart and invested in a *ballistic hardcore tactical case*. Now, my phone could survive drops of twelve feet onto concrete. Being a klutz, I tended to break a lot of stuff, including pinky toes. Sometimes I even dropped stuff *on* my pinky toe and broke two things at once. Don't try that at home, kids, I'm a trained professional.

I managed to answer on the fourth ring. "Hello?"

"Hey Jamie, it's Jess, why are you out of breath?"

"Just doing a little exercise," I said, because crawling around on the floor looking for your cell phone counts. "I was so sorry to hear about Clarence," I added. "Do they know what happened?" I stood by the window watching the sun set in fiery-orange streaks and purple-tinged clouds. It seemed like the perfect backdrop for a discussion about life and death.

"They think it was his heart, but they don't really know," Jessie said. "At least he didn't suffer. But I called to talk about something more pleasant. How would you like to do a little side work?"

"You mean, like bathing dogs at the shelter? Sure, I can help."

"Not washing dogs, silly, *real* work, lawyer work."

"If it's a messy divorce," I said, "I'll pass. I'm kind of burnt out right now, to tell you the truth."

Jessie laughed. "Nothing like that, this is easy money."

"My favorite kind. Go on."

"La Vida Boca has a lawyer come once a month to explain living wills, health care surrogates and family powers of attorney to the residents and then help them fill out the forms," Jessie explained. "He's retiring and they asked me if I knew anyone."

"That guy has been ripping them off," I said. "Those forms are available online for free, along with instructions."

"Nobody's ripping anyone off," Jessie said calmly. "You

46

clearly haven't spent much time with old people. How many of them do you think even have computers? Anyway, it's a benefit for the residents but it also helps the facility. If residents have living wills and health surrogate forms on file, La Vida Boca doesn't have to hunt for next of kin when things happen."

"But what about competency? How is the lawyer supposed to judge their mental capacity?"

"Not to worry. People diagnosed with dementia can't participate," Jessie reassured me.

"Why every month?" I asked.

"Because new residents are constantly moving in, if you catch my drift."

"Got it," I said. "Alright, I'll do it. If nothing else it'll give me a break from my divorce clients." Those good vibes I'd sent out to the universe were already bouncing back.

"Don't you want to know what it pays?" Jessie teased.

"You bet I do."

"Does six hundred a month sound good?

"You bet it does."

"And they provide lunch," Jessie added.

"No thanks," I said. "Their cook thinks salt is a four letter word."

"You could always bring your own."

I laughed. "If I bring the salt, will you bring the Margaritas?"

\*\*\*

It just so happened that I had a hearing scheduled for Thursday morning in West Palm. Since La Vida Boca was on the way, I decided to stop in afterward to complete the paperwork for my new job. I'd hoped to do it in the comfort of my office and e-mail it in, but Wilma, the director, wanted a face-to-face. On the phone, she'd said *come anytime*, she was *always there*, but it turns out that being *there* and being *available* were not synonyms in Miss Wilma's lexicon.

When I arrived at ten o'clock the lobby was strangely

empty. Where were the residents? Breakfast was over, it was too soon for lunch--maybe they were playing Bingo. Glenda the receptionist didn't recognize me from my previous visit but I didn't take it personally. I did take it personally, though, when she told me the director couldn't be disturbed. It seemed like Wilma was starting our new relationship by playing hard to get. Well, I wasn't leaving without seeing her because if I walked out that door I wasn't coming back. It's not like I needed this job. At least Wilma's picture was on the wall so I knew who to look for as I hunted her down.

I checked the Bingo hall, the card room, the lunch room, and the library, but no Wilma. What bothered me more were the missing residents. Where was everybody? I passed the exercise room and the movie theater (unfamiliar territory) but stopped when I heard organ music coming from behind large double doors. I quietly turned the knob so I could poke my head in and check it out. The huge room was fully occupied. Then I realized where I was. This was the chapel and the service was about to begin. I was right on time for Clarence Petersen's memorial.

# Chapter Seventeen

Now I understood why Wilma was unavailable, but I still didn't want to come back another day. I was about to exit the chapel when I heard someone call my name.

"Jamie, over here." The voice was coming from my left.

Although she wasn't dressed for gardening, I still recognized her.

"Nice to see you again, Jodi," I said.

Jodi Martin gave me a friendly smile and patted the empty seat next to her.

I shook my head. "Oh no, I'm not staying,"

Just then, the organ music stopped and the minister asked everyone to be seated. I wanted to leave, but didn't want to be rude. Then I realized I didn't care what these people thought; they couldn't shame me into attending a stranger's funeral. I looked for Jessie in the crowd, but she wasn't there--why would she be? My only reason for staying would be to catch Wilma on her way out. While patience wasn't my forte, I'd learned that sometimes the long way around is the fastest. Like when you try to pass a slow car only to find yourself behind them again at the red light. What I'm saying is some things are beyond our control. My new philosophy was to suck it up and smile because life's too short and, if you're lucky, you'll be calling the Bingo numbers when you're a hundred and two. With a sigh, I took a seat next to Jodi.

"I'm going to miss Clarence," she said. "He was a lot of fun."

"Really?" I was starting to wish I'd met him.

"Oh, yeah," Jodi's hazel eyes shone. "He was the king of practical jokes. One time he brought *delicious* caramel apples to the potluck dinner..."

"And?"

"They were caramel onions!" Jodi laughed.

"Funny," I said.

49

"Another time, he put whoopee cushions on everyone's chair."

"Of course he did," I said. "It sounds like old age is a return to childhood, à la Benjamin Button."

"I suppose," Jodi agreed, "except nobody here ever turns into Brad Pitt."

"What a shame," I said.

We shared a discreet laugh and then settled down for the sermon which was mercifully short and mildly inspiring. The Unitarian minister was a pleasant man who had come well-stocked with generic platitudes and words of comfort, but it was clear he was a rent-a-rev who'd never met the dearly departed. I swore that my send-off would be different. When it was my time, I wanted a big-ass party where people told funny stories--and they'd better damn well know me. While I hoped to die a hero, the odds were I'd choke on a sandwich tripping over my cat. At least that would be a good story to get the party started.

When the minister finished, he called Clarence Jr. to the podium. A trim man in his fifties walked purposefully towards the microphone. After fishing note cards from his jacket pocket, he donned a pair of half-moon reading glasses and cleared his throat.

"Thank-you for coming," he began. "My dad would've loved seeing you all here--mainly so he could try out his new jokes. As you know, my father wasn't very discriminating--good jokes, bad jokes, it didn't matter, he just liked to have fun." Everyone laughed and Clarence Jr. smiled back at the audience.

"Being a prankster," he continued, "was actually my dad's second career. Everyone who ever visited my parents' apartment admired their exquisite antique furniture. My dad used to be an antiques dealer and he was the best in the business. He opened Petersen's Antiques when I was just a baby and I'm proud to say the business is still thriving today. Dad used to say that collecting antiques was like being a world traveler and a time traveler all in one. He told me that the pieces whispered their stories in his ear, but the truth was he did tons of research and he did it the old-fashioned way because there was no internet back then. He had an eye for rare books, fine furniture, art, and china. The only thing he wouldn't buy

50

was vintage clothing. He said he didn't have the figure for it."

Everyone chuckled at that, even me. Then Clarence Jr.'s expression turned serious.

"I know everyone would agree that my father was a good man and a great father and husband." Then he choked up and said, "I'll miss you, Dad," and walked back to his seat with his head bowed.

I thought the service was over, but then Clarence's widow, Shirley, stood up. Her son rose from his chair and whispered something in her ear, but she shook him off with an angry gesture before marching over to the podium. Her snow-white hair and bent posture made her look fragile, but her blue eyes were fierce when she turned to face us.

"Let's stop pretending everything was alright," she said. "Everyone knows my husband hadn't been himself for months and one of you knows the reason why. Somebody here betrayed Clarence's trust and it destroyed him." She pointed a bony finger at the crowd. "You know who you are!"

# Chapter Eighteen

Shirley Petersen had kicked over a hornet's nest with her accusation. In no time, the quiet hum of the room had escalated to an outraged buzzing and people were shouting to be heard above the din. Funeral decorum flew out the window and Clarence's memorial service became a free-for-all.

"Who was it, Shirley? Tell us."

"Clarence seemed fine to me…"

"Shirley's lost her mind!"

"Will someone tell me what's going on?"

"WHAT DID SHE SAY? I TURNED MY HEARING AID OFF."

But Shirley had no intention of responding to anyone. After she finished her shocking speech she exited through the back with a bewildered Clarence Jr. close behind.

Jodi Martin and I were gaping at the spectacle when Jodi leaned over to make a comment. "Can you believe what's going on here? We haven't seen this much drama since Millie and Ruth had a food fight in the dining room. That was pretty nasty, let me tell you. Chocolate pudding is permanently off the menu because of them."

I wrinkled my nose in sympathy for her lost pudding. "So, what do you think Shirley meant?" I was curious, I'll admit it.

She shrugged. "No idea, but I imagine the Book Club could tell us. They know all the gossip at La Vida Boca."

"Let me know what you hear," I said, but I was thinking that if anyone knew what was going on, it would be Clarence's buddies, the Card Sharks. Maybe Jessie could ask her Uncle Teddy.

With all the excitement I'd nearly forgotten why I was there in the first place--to see Wilma, the director. I scanned the crowd (a crowd which should have been disbursing, but wasn't) and spotted a dyed-red bouffant crossing the room. Lucky for me, Wilma hadn't changed her hairstyle since the seventies--or at least since they'd hung her picture in the lobby, which may well have been the seventies. To make my way over to her I had to squeeze past the residents who weren't budging, not even the mobile ones. When gentle prodding didn't work, I used my elbows to encourage them to get a move on. My elbows can be pretty darn persuasive. As I inched towards Wilma, I kept my eye on her hair, blazing like a four-alarm fire. The woman wasn't subtle, I could tell that already. Shame on me for forming an opinion before we'd even met. I mean, I'd only seen her hair, but that image was burned into my retinas forever.

When I finally reached her, I found a middle-aged debutante in a loud floral dress that clashed with her hair. She wasn't tall, but her bouffant gave her height and presence, and her vivid lipstick commanded attention. Her expression was one of perpetual annoyance. Although I was standing right in front of her, she somehow managed not to see me, which was quite a feat. I must've forgotten to remove my invisibility cloak--or maybe she was just plain rude. I would have understood it had I been wearing my usual ensemble of beat-up jeans and a t-shirt, but I had on my best power suit and looked like a real attorney. What was the deal with this lady? After observing her for a few minutes (the advantage of being invisible) I figured it out. Wilma saw herself as the queen bee and the rest of us as drones, expendable and interchangeable, serving at her pleasure, useful only when she needed something. I watched in fascination as she confronted an aide struggling to move a wheelchair.

"For heaven's sake, young lady, what are you doing?" Wilma demanded, arms crossed over her floral chest. "Do we pay you to push empty wheelchairs around? Where are you supposed to be?"

"No ma'am, I mean, yes ma'am, I mean--" the aide sputtered

"--It's a simple question," Wilma said, shooting daggers out of her eyes.

As soothing as the chapel was with its non-denominational stained glass and inspirational décor, it did nothing to calm the flustered aide, so I decided to help. It was time I introduced myself anyway. Taking two steps forward, I plopped myself down in the wheelchair and, just like that, I was visible again.

"Whew! These heels are killing me," I said, giving the aide a side wink before offering Wilma my sweetest smile. Charm and disarm, that's my motto.

It was the director's turn to look confused, as if she didn't know whether to smile back at me or call security.

I stood up before she made the wrong choice and extended my hand. "You must be Wilma," I said. "I recognize you from your picture, although I must say it doesn't do you justice. You're the person I'm here to see."

Once I'd stepped out of the chair, the aide saw a chance to escape and she took it. My good deed for the day was done. Wilma was too busy sizing me up to notice.

"And you are...?" She asked, eyes narrowed.

I guess my honest face and kissing up hadn't impressed her. Well, I'd worked tough rooms before and I don't back away from a challenge. If it's true that everyone is a salesman, then this lady was going to buy what I was selling. She just didn't know it yet.

I smiled. "I'm Jamie Quinn, your new lawyer, we spoke on the phone. You asked me to come in to do the paperwork."

"Why, of course you are!" Wilma gushed, her Southern accent thick as honey. "Welcome, welcome. I've been expecting you," she lied. Then a look of bewilderment crossed her face. "Were you at the memorial? Did you know Clarence?"

I nodded solemnly. "He was a friend of a friend."

She brightened. "It seems like you're already part of the family. That's our motto, you know. *You're family when you're living La Vida Boca.*"

"That's nice," I said. "Did you have to pay royalties to Ricky Martin?" I almost started laughing. Living La Vida Loca sounded like way more fun than living La Vida Boca but the joke was wasted on Wilma.

As we walked towards the office, we talked about my duties. I assured her I would explain the forms to the residents and assist those who were interested.

She stopped in her tracks. "I'm afraid you've misunderstood your role," she said in a bossy tone. "You need to *highly encourage* them to fill out the forms. We want every resident to have those forms on file."

"It sounds like you're looking for someone else," I said. "Someone who doesn't follow the rules of ethics set out by the Florida Bar. I wish you luck in finding that person." I held out my hand to bid her farewell.

Wilma was rattled. "No, no, that's certainly not what I meant, I, uh, just wanted you to understand our position, that's all."

I nodded. "Fair enough. Let's talk salary, shall we?"

"Yes," she agreed, "let's do that. The pay is five hundred per session, payable monthly."

"Interesting," I said. "I was under the impression it paid seven hundred fifty per session, considering that that would be a discount from my hourly rate and there's travel involved. Not many lawyers make house calls, you know. Not even doctors do that anymore."

Wilma sighed, as if it pained her to dig so deep into her limited budget. "I suppose I could go up to five seventy-five…"

"Let's split the difference," I said. "Six fifty and you have a deal."

With an air of resignation, she agreed.

I congratulated her. "You drive a hard bargain, Wilma."

# Chapter Nineteen

Before I left, Wilma insisted we schedule my first 'educational seminar' for the following Monday. It was short notice but I could make it work if our receptionist helped me put the documents together. If she wasn't too busy working for Nelda, that is.

It was way past lunchtime and I'd skipped breakfast, but I didn't want to stop because the day was half over and I hadn't been to the office yet. I'd gone from home to the courthouse to La Vida Boca where I'd attended a memorial service that wasn't on my day planner. Finding a drive-thru was the sensible solution if only veggie burgers were as ubiquitous as beef. As I drove down U.S. 1 in search of lunch, I turned on the radio and sang along with *Owner of a Lonely Heart*. I was having a blast until I realized how easily that could become my new theme song and I turned it off. That's right, I said no to *Yes*.

I was so hungry I couldn't lower my expectations fast enough. When I saw a Pollo Tropical on the right I began to imagine steamy black beans and fluffy white rice with a dash of hot sauce having a party in my mouth, so I drove to the window and ordered a large side of each, with flan for dessert. Custard with caramelized sugar is impossible for mere mortals to resist.

I was about to park the car so I could shovel the beans and rice down the hatch when my phone rang. "Worst timing ever, Broussard," I said. "If you talk, I'll listen, but I have to eat or I'll get cranky."

Duke laughed. "Sounds like that ship has sailed, Darlin."

"Hilarious," I said. "Start talking or listen to me chew. Your choice."

"You know," he said, "I like being a P.I.--"

"--Congrats on making the right career choice."

"I thought you were gonna listen and not talk?" Duke said.

"Yeah, yeah. Go on."

"*As I was sayin'*, I like being a P.I., but I didn't sign up to be a dang librarian. All I do these days is plow through boxes of papers and read until my eyes are bloodshot."

I paused between bites; I had to come up for air anyway. "What's going on, Duke? Are you being audited? I told you not paying taxes would bite you in the backside one day."

"What are you smoking, girl? I'm talking about Jeff Rappaport, my new client, your old client. Is it coming back to you now?"

I opened the container of flan and inhaled blissfully. "Sorry, not thinking straight, I must've been delirious from hunger. I get it, you're going through Jeff's papers. Did you find anything?"

"Not much, but I'm still digging. I found a copy of the insurance policy, so at least I know when Earl bought the painting."

"That's something! Good work, Duke. What's next?" I asked.

"Try to follow the money, I guess. His bank was bought out a while back but the account was too old to research anyway."

I licked the last bit of caramel off my fingers. "Is the insurance company still around? They might have some info on the purchase. You could also research that certificate of authenticity Jeff has."

"Not bad, Ms. Esquire, I'll look into that. But I'd rather be tailing somebody or doing some real P.I. stuff."

That made me laugh. "P.I. work isn't all fun and games and being a pretend rapper, you know."

"Yeah, I guess sometimes you have to pay the bills," Duke agreed.

"Some of us pay our bills all the time," I said. "Now, get going, Marmaduke Broussard, III."

\*\*\*

With a full belly and a guilty conscience, I went back to my office to try to do a little work. Considering how unproductive I'd been and how long it would take me to drive from Boca to Hollywood, I decided to listen to the Probate seminar I'd downloaded. I really tried to pay attention, but it was so boring my mind kept wandering. I thought about Kip, how I promised we'd talk, and how I was dreading it. I wondered if I'd get to meet my father soon and whether I'd like Nicaragua, the Land of Lakes and Volcanoes. My dad told me it was beautiful with lots of nature and seven hundred species of birds.

Suddenly, a loud honk jolted me out of my daydream. The blast wasn't meant for me but still produced a rush of adrenaline that made me pay attention to my surroundings. I realized I was driving through Dania, a small town lined with little stores and restaurants just north of Hollywood. One particular block held about a dozen antique shops that brought back a slew of memories. When I was eight, my mom and I had decided to start a collection together. We chose antique bells because they were sturdy and inexpensive and because we could have fun with them, arranging them by size or by sound. Whenever our favorite songs came on the radio, we would grab a bell and play along. On Saturdays, we liked to go to breakfast and then drive to Dania to hunt for bells. We even called it 'the hunt'. My favorite store had a fleur-de-lis on the front window. The owner was a nice man with a Swedish accent who told silly jokes and pulled quarters out of my ear. Whenever a new shipment of antiques came in, he would always set aside the bells for us in a separate drawer. After my mom died, I kept the bell collection. It still resides on the windowsills in my house, right where my mother left it.

When I saw the store with the fleur-de-lis on the glass, I had to stop; it was like a sign after all these years. I parked my car around the corner and went in. When I opened the door, it jingled just the way I remembered it. Then, I had to do an about-face, I couldn't believe my eyes. Above the fleur-de-lis etched on the glass was the name of the store which I'm sure I'd seen a hundred times but it had never meant anything to me before. Now, the gold letters linked my past to my present in the strangest of ways. The store I was about to enter was Petersen's Antiques. To my surprise, I realized I did know Clarence Petersen.

58

# Chapter Twenty

The store smelled just the way I remembered it, a comforting bouquet of furniture polish, musty books, cedar, and potpourri. Instantly, I was eight years old again, butterflies in my stomach, looking for hidden treasures. I don't know if other kids loved antique stores as much as I did, but I know that if history class were taught in an antique store we'd all be experts. I remembered how patiently Mr. Petersen would answer my barrage of questions--what was this called, what did it do, where did it come from. Everything there was old, but it was all new to me. I learned that before washing machines were invented, clothes were scrubbed by hand on aluminum washboards (glass boards for delicates), then fed through a wringer before being hung up to dry. I learned that in the 1930's people used wooden ice boxes with large blocks of ice to keep food from rotting, and that ice had to be harvested from cold places before being transported by train--a big business until refrigerators came along. Often when Mr. Petersen would explain an item to me, my mom would chime in with, "See how easy we have it now, Jamie?" No matter how many times she said it, I still hated cleaning my room.

Once I had the lowdown on the basics, I could focus on my favorites, like the delicate porcelain dolls with their long lashes and pretty glass eyes. I wondered if the little girls who owned them had passed them down to their daughters and how the dolls had ended up at Petersen's. I remembered an ornate walnut dining table with knobby legs in the center of the store where I used to sit and imagine a family having dinner, the parents discussing their day, passing the food while the kids horsed around. In my mind, it looked like a Norman Rockwell painting and I wanted to be in it. As an only child, I loved the idea of a loud, bustling family.

Walking around the store, I was surprised at how little had changed in almost thirty years. Aside from a small sign on the door that said "Follow us on Facebook", Petersen's looked basically the same. Different inventory and new carpet didn't take away the feeling that my mom, Sue, could've been just out of sight, bending over a box of vinyl records and humming *Moon River*. I was standing there admiring a gold mirror when I heard someone behind me say, "Let me know if you need any help." I turned around, but the only other person in the store was a lanky black guy with close-cropped hair. He was college-age, with an open, sincere face like my cousin Adam.

Puzzled, I asked, "Do you work here?"

He laughed shyly. "No, I'm just extremely helpful. Sorry, I'm Darren and yes, I work here."

"Really?" I joked. "You seem kinda young to be an expert on all things antique. I believe I have clothes in my closet older than you."

"Interesting analogy," he said, with the confidence of a debate team captain. "But can your clothes appraise the value of Star Trek and Star Wars collectibles?"

I laughed appreciatively. "Only the ones I wore to Comic-Con, they're super nerdy. The rest of my clothes always make fun of them."

"They're just jealous," he said.

"Obviously," I said. "Can you blame them?" I glanced around the store. "Where are these cool collectibles anyway? I must've missed them."

"Sadly, we don't have any at the moment," he replied, genuine regret on his boyish face. "Is that what you're looking for?"

I sensed that if I said yes, I would be pulled into a virtual Star Trek convention, and that wasn't why I was there. I wasn't sure why I was there. How could I explain my nostalgia to someone too young to understand? Then I perked up.

"Do you have any hand bells? I used to buy them here a long time ago."

All business, Darren nodded and turned on his long legs toward a display case by the register where half a dozen bells kept company on a strip of rich green velvet. There was a Victorian lady in a wide dress holding a fan, a small Dutch woman made of brass, and a plain silver bell topped with a flying Pegasus. I felt a flush of happiness.

"I'll take them all," I said.

"Don't you want to know how much they are?"

"Are they less than twenty dollars each?"

Darren nodded.

"Then wrap them up, my Trekkie friend, this is your big sale of the day."

After congratulating me on my excellent choice without a hint of irony, Darren pulled out a box of tissue paper and meticulously wrapped each bell. The tissue paper had a fleur-de-lis pattern identical to the one on the window. Suddenly, I noticed the fleur-de-lis was everywhere, every price tag, every sign, it was even on the wallpaper. *Pay attention much, Jamie?* I turned around when Darren asked me to sign the credit card slip and that's when I saw them--business cards offering fine art appraisals. It occurred to me that Duke could bring in the fake Chagall for an expert opinion since he didn't have much else to go on. It might give him a lead.

"Hey, tell me about this art appraiser. Is he any good?"

Darren handed me my bag. "Of course! He's the best in the business."

"Normally, I'd take your word for it," I said, "but I need someone who can appraise paintings. What are this guy's credentials?"

With an air of gravitas I found adorable in a twenty-year-old, Darren informed me that their appraiser was a member of The Appraisers Association of America, The American Association of Museums, certified in Appraisal Studies, and held a graduate degree in art history from a prestigious university.

I clapped my hands. "Excellent! Did you forget anything?"

Darren broke down and smiled. "He was also on *Antiques Roadshow.*"

"Good enough for me." I said, pocketing a business card.

After inhaling the aroma of yesteryear once more, I left Petersen's Antiques, a bag of jingling bells beneath my arm. On the short drive back to my office, I thought about how odd it was that I'd gone to Clarence Petersen's memorial service without realizing who he was and what he'd meant to me, and how much he had enriched my childhood with his kindness, patience and magic tricks.

61

I took a moment to mourn his passing, better late than never. My thoughts were interrupted by the Probate CD droning on in the background which I'd forgotten to shut off. The lecture was extremely dry and boring until it became unintentionally amusing. I didn't know this, but the personal representative of an estate is required to file one last income tax return for the decedent. Thus, two of life's certainties, death and taxes go together hand in hand at the end. It made me laugh to think that someday, when he wasn't around to see it, Duke would finally have to file that tax return.

# Chapter Twenty-One

It was three o'clock when I finally made it to the office. I was ashamed to admit that my only billable time for the day had been a brief court appearance in the morning. I was so good at slacking off I could teach a class. Fortunately, there was still time to do some work--as long as nobody interrupted me. After shedding my jacket and kicking off my shoes, I shut the door, grabbed a cold drink from the breakroom fridge and picked up the closest file. I wiggled my grateful toes in the soft carpet and began to prep for mediation. I was just starting my notes when the intercom buzzed. I'd forgotten to tell the receptionist I didn't want to be disturbed.

"Yes, Nicole?"

"Hey Jamie, a delivery guy's been calling for you all day and he's on the phone again."

I wasn't expecting any deliveries. While I ordered almost everything online, it all went to my house. "I don't understand," I said. "Why do I need to talk to him? If he has something to deliver, tell him to just do it." Sheesh! Why did everyone need me to hold their hand?

Nicole sighed. "You don't want to talk to him?"

"Not really. Also, can you make sure he's legit and not some angry ex-husband with a Molotov cocktail. You can't be too paranoid, right?"

Nicole hesitated. "Should I be worried?"

"Nobody's out to get me that I know of, if that helps."

"It doesn't," she said tersely. "And we need to talk about my raise." She hung up before I could say *why don't you ask Nelda?*

I went back to my file and started organizing the financial docs. Not ten minutes later the intercom buzzed again. I considered ignoring it, but Nicole was in no mood and, stupid me, I hadn't told her not to disturb me after the first time.

"What's up, Nicole?"

"Jamie, you need to come out here right now!" Then she giggled and hung up.

I wondered who worked for whom in this office but did as I was told. I even put my shoes on before marching over to the reception area determined to discuss some ground rules with Nicole. As I rounded the corner, my jaw dropped and then I couldn't stop smiling. Standing there were four mustachioed men in identical candy-cane-striped vests, white shirts and black pants, straw boaters on their heads, snazzy red bowties around their necks. It took me a minute to realize they were a barbershop quartet!

"Here she is," Nicole announced gleefully.

Nelda was standing behind Nicole with her secretary and paralegal, all of them beaming like it was Christmas in July. On cue, the four gentlemen took off their hats and held them over their hearts.

The youngest one stepped forward and said, "Jamie, these songs were specially selected for you by Kip with love."

He blew into a pitch pipe and they began to serenade me in four-part harmony. The first song was *I Only Have Eyes for You*. When they finished, I was tearing up about my wonderful boyfriend and the girls were clapping and whistling. Then the quartet launched into three more songs: *I Found a Million Dollar Baby*, *You're Nobody Till Somebody Loves You*, and *Love is Here to Stay*, before they stopped to take a breather. The bass in the group, an older man with pomaded hair, stepped forward and asked Nicole to hand him a dozen pink roses from the desk which he then presented to me with a flourish. For the grand finale, the foursome sang *I'll Be Seeing You* and added a little soft-shoe to their performance. They held the last note for an incredibly long time and we clapped until our hands hurt. Afterwards, we cajoled them to stay but they couldn't, they had songs to sing. I marveled at how they had found their calling-- making people happy while doing what they loved. I definitely took a wrong turn somewhere.

"That Kip is a keeper!" said Nelda after they'd gone.

"Does he have any brothers?" Nicole asked hopefully.

I laughed. "Yes, he's a keeper and yes, he has a brother in New York."

"Have a nice life, ladies," Nicole joked, "I'm off to the Big Apple. Wait, hang on a sec." She pulled a mirror from her purse and refreshed her glossy lipstick. "Now, I'm ready."

"You look fabulous," Nelda said in her slight Brazilian accent. "Good luck! We'll follow you on Instant Gram."

Shaking her head, Nelda's hip, young secretary took her by the arm and led her away. "It's *Instagram*, Nelda. Don't worry, Grandma, we'll keep you on track."

I waltzed back to my office singing in one-part harmony, which I guess you would call the melody. Nothing recognizable, just snippets from each song I'd heard all mashed together. My almost-fiancé Kip was the bomb and I couldn't wait another minute to tell him. I rushed to my desk to Skype with him but he wasn't logged on--no surprise since it was seven a.m. in Queensland and he was probably on his way to work. I called his cell but it went to voicemail, so, after listening to his sexy voice, I left a message proclaiming him boyfriend of the year. Then I texted him.

*I think you must love me a lot, Kip Simons*

*You're not sure?* He texted back. *Didn't those guys sing the right songs?*

I typed a row of hearts. *Oh, yes! All the right songs. You won the love of every woman in my office, as a matter of fact.*

*Excellent! Do I have a fan club now, like Justin Bieber?*

*More like George Clooney,* I replied.

*Yeah, George and I hang out all the time.*

*That's what I heard,* I texted. *Hey, I'm sorry I got mad at you...*

*Babe, I'm the one who's sorry. You know I can't wait to see you, right?*

My heart soared in response. I could never quit this guy. *All I know is I can't wait to see you,* I answered. *Are you coming home?*

I assumed he was typing furiously because the three dots kept repeating for several minutes and then they stopped. And then they started and stopped again.

*Kip?*

He finally answered. *It's complicated. I can't explain it over text, but I promise I'll be home as soon as I can. Okay?*

*It depends on how you define home,* I wrote. *You mean Hollywood, Florida, right?*

*I mean wherever you are. That's my home.*

I was choking up. *I love you, my crazy tree-hugger.*
*And I love you, Jamie. Don't forget, okay?*

After we said good-bye, I leaned back in my chair, eyes closed, savoring the moment. I felt lighter than air, a balloon carried by the breeze, content with the world. I was about to put my phone away when I noticed that Kip had texted me again. Still smiling, I typed in my password so I could read the message and then I stopped smiling. I don't know who Kip meant to text, but his message clearly wasn't meant for me--because it was about me. It read:

*Don't worry, I didn't tell Jamie what's going on. She'll find out soon enough.*

# Chapter Twenty-Two

Just because you're paranoid doesn't mean your boyfriend isn't keeping secrets! What was Kip up to? Who was he texting? Did he hire the barbershop quartet to ease his guilty conscience? Of all the people I knew, who could he be in contact with? The list was short--basically anyone who had called when he was looking for me: Aunt Peg, Adam, Grace, Ana Maria and Duke. There was no way Adam could keep a secret, so he was out. Aunt Peg could keep a secret forever if she had to, but would Kip confide in her? No, cross her off. Kip barely knew Ana Maria, so that left Duke and Grace. I decided to take the direct approach and call Duke.

"Hey, Broussard," I said when he picked up. "Do you know something I don't?"

He sounded like he was choking on a drink, but recovered quickly. "Darlin', the things I know that you don't could fill a book, but I'm available for private lessons. First lesson's free!" He laughed like the happiest guy at happy hour, which he usually was.

"Seriously," I said, shutting my office door. "Is there something going on? And if there were, would you tell me?"

Duke lowered his voice to a hoarse whisper. "You mean, like some kinda conspiracy? Look, if somebody's bothering you, Ms. Esquire, you just tell me who it is and I'll kick his ass."

"Appreciate the offer, Duke, but you have no idea what I'm talking about, do you?"

"Not a clue. But I'm intrigued, I really am," he said. "Now, you gonna tell me or what?"

"Nothing to tell, thanks anyway. Don't drink and drive."

He laughed. "Don't you worry, I'm sure one of these lovely ladies will drive me home--" A high-pitched squeal came through the phone.

"Bye, Duke." I ended the call.

That left Grace and I knew she'd never hurt me. If Kip were coming home and wanted to surprise me, he would need Grace's help. If that were the case, I didn't want to spoil it by

67

confronting them. What else could it be? I hated being out of the loop and I couldn't stand it that Kip was keeping secrets. Whoever the message was intended for obviously hadn't received it and Kip wouldn't realize his mistake until he went to text me again. There was a wildly remote possibility that it was something terrible, like Kip had a girlfriend and was planning to break up with me. A cloud of jealousy fogged my brain, but picturing the barbershop quartet singing their hearts out calmed me down. I'd just have to wait--not patiently, of course, that wasn't my style--but I wouldn't obsess either, I would lock this problem in a box and walk away. When Kip realized what he'd done, he'd have to come up with an explanation--and it had better be a damn good one.

\*\*\*

It had been a long day and a tiring one, considering how little I'd accomplished. Before packing up to leave I sent a quick e-mail to Jessie about Shirley Petersen's outburst and asked her if Uncle Teddy might know who betrayed Clarence. The plot thickens! Dun dun dun!

When I got home, I checked my mailbox and found another surprise waiting for me. This one was wrapped in brown paper and shaped like a book. That's because it was a book--one I desperately needed, according to my friend Grace. The card read: *I expect some awesome Christmas presents this year! Xoxo.* Inside was a classic tome essential for pet owners everywhere: "Crafting with Cat Hair: Cute Handicrafts to Make with Your Cat". Laughing, I went inside to feed His Majesty after which I planned to send Grace a special book of her own: "Frog or Prince? The Smart Girl's Guide to Boyfriends".

# Chapter Twenty-Three

To cap off my week, I went to a mediation on Friday that was surreal. It started out fine, almost pleasant, which should've been my first clue. The mediator served bagels and coffee, the opposing counsel was a decent guy, and the parties seemed reasonable. It was a short marriage, no kids, and it didn't take us long to divide the property and allocate the debts. We were wrapping things up (or so we thought), congratulating each other on a job well done when my client said to his client "I'll be over to pick up Roxy and Rico this afternoon", to which her future ex-husband replied, "Like hell, you will."

To be clear, under Florida law, dogs are *property*; they are not in any legal sense considered *children*. Nevertheless, the five of us worked well into the afternoon, incurring over a thousand dollars in legal fees *per side*, drafting a *shared custody agreement* for two mutts that had been adopted for free. We even established a holiday visitation schedule and doggie health insurance, I kid you not. That is why family lawyers never say "Now, I've seen it all" because they know they'd be lying.

I shouldn't complain--it's not like I do physical labor or anything--but mediating is exhausting and when it's over I don't have two brain cells to rub together. Once, I even forgot to pick up Mr. Paws from the vet and he almost had to spend the night. He was not pleased and, let me tell you, that cat can carry a grudge forever. You don't have to ask Mr. Paws how he really feels, he'll swat you in the head just for looking at him.

Because I couldn't think straight after four hours of discussing whether Roxy and Rico would spend Thanksgiving with "Mummy" or "Daddy", I forgot to make copies of the information packet for my upcoming seminar at La Vida Boca. What I mean is I forgot to ask Nicole to do it. What a waste of a barbershop quartet! All that good will would be gone by Monday. No way was I staying late on a Friday night to copy and collate, even if it meant taking a weekend trip to the office. I just didn't have it in me. All I wanted was to go home and plant myself on the sofa, remote control in one hand, glass of wine in the other. Then my cell rang and I saw that it was one of my favorite people.

"Hey James, TGIF! You have plans tonight?"

I sat back down and propped my feet on the desk. "As a matter of fact, Gracie, I do. See if you can guess."

She laughed. "Hmmm, does it involve making cute handicrafts with your cat?"

"Bingo! Christmas is only five months away and Mr. Paws is quite the temperamental artist, as you know. One wrong word and he storms off in a huff."

"Or scratches your eyes out," she added.

"Judge the art, not the artist, Grace."

"We're still talking about a cat, right?"

"I'm not sure," I said, "my brain clocked out a few hours ago. What's up, my BFF?"

"I was wondering--do you want to check out a new brewery in Fort Lauderdale? They have games and food trucks."

"But do they have beer?" I joked.

"They have kegs and kegs of the stuff--with flavors like coffee, and peanut butter and jelly."

"Call me old-fashioned," I said, "but I like beer-flavored beer. Do they have any of that?"

"Tell you what," Grace said, "If they don't, we'll go somewhere else. Deal?"

"Deal. Pick me up? I don't feel like driving."

"Sure! You at work?" she asked.

"Yup."

"We'll see you in fifteen."

"Who's *we*?" I said. But she'd already hung up.

Grace had tricked me. If I weren't so tired, I would have asked the obvious--who else is going? Now, I was stuck. Making small talk with my frenemy was not my idea of fun on a good day. The worst part was not being able to leave when I wanted to. But I really was too exhausted to drive and drinking would only make it worse, even if the beer *was* infused with coffee. Yuck!

70

***

"Hello, Quinn," Nick said pleasantly enough after I hopped into the back seat of Grace's Prius. "It's been a while. How have you managed to stay out of trouble so long?"

"Funny, Nick. As you may recall, it hasn't been *that* long since Grace and I were trapped in a sauna."

"Worst spa day ever!" Grace chimed in as she maneuvered through rush hour traffic.

"Yeah," I said, "we were literally sweating to death. Hey, next time let's get stuck in an elevator, okay?"

"Agreed," Grace said, grinning at me through the rear-view mirror.

Nick was incredulous, "Are you looking for trouble, Quinn?"

I shook my head. "I don't have to, Nick, trouble always finds me."

"Can't argue with that," he said.

After Grace parked we waited together at the light to cross the street.

"I just love it when you two get along!" she said, throwing her arms around our shoulders. It wasn't quite a group hug, but still too close for comfort.

I had to laugh. "You know, when I first met this guy, he pissed me off so much I wanted to dump hot coffee on his fancy suit. Now, we're going out for drinks together. Hard to believe."

"You forgot the part about how he's dating your friend," Grace added, nudging me. "That's the best part."

"No," I said, "the best part is that I can dump a coffee-flavored beer on him later and pretend it was an accident. As they say, revenge is a dish best served cold--ice cold is even better."

Nick cracked a rare smile. "Good luck finding a ride home, Quinn. You could always take an Uber."

"One of us may be taking an Uber, but it won't be me. You shouldn't test Grace's loyalties like that, Nick--and so early in the relationship, too."

"If you two don't knock it off," Grace laughed, "you'll both

71

be taking an Uber."

We entered the crowded brewery where I looked in vain for somewhere to sit, but Grace had a different plan and guided us through a side door to a quiet enclave outside where there was an empty table.

"This is good," I said, scooting into the booth across from them. "If we could only get a beer, my life would be complete. I can't wait until Nick starts drinking and spills all his secrets. Won't that be entertaining?" I smiled at Grace.

Nick took off his expensive jacket and loosened his tie a smidge, but he still looked like a state attorney. It was the haircut and the way he squared his shoulders that gave it away. What did Grace see in him, anyway? Sure, he was handsome with his chiseled features and a body that regularly hit the gym, but he was about as much fun as watching the weather channel.

"You'll have to find your entertainment elsewhere, Quinn, I don't drink."

I smacked my hand down on the wooden table. "Not cool, Nick. I'm going to get drunk and spill my secrets and you'll be sitting there taking notes! Seriously, Grace?"

She took my hand like she was my nurse and I was her unhinged patient. "It's okay, Jamie, don't worry. Nothing you say tonight can be used against you in a court of law." Grace flipped her long dark hair over her shoulder and then kissed her boyfriend on the cheek. "Nick knows not to mess with my BFF. I'm going to grab some menus. You two behave while I'm gone, you hear?" She gave us a warning look and swished out of the booth, steady on her high heels.

"Don't blow this, Dimitropoulos," I said as we watched her walk away.

"I'm trying not to," he said sincerely. His classic Greek profile was softened by a look of genuine affection. I don't know why I was so surprised.

"Wow, Nick, you do have a heart. All this time, I thought you were an android sent to spy on us by our alien overlords. I hate it when I'm wrong."

"Surely you must be used to it by now, Quinn," Nick said

with a half-smile.

"You crack yourself up, don't you?" I joked. "Hey, aren't you two supposed to be at a meet and greet tonight?"

He nodded. "Apparently, my opponent was so intimidated by me that he canceled. Not really, it's being rescheduled." Then he gave me a quizzical look. "I ran into a friend of yours yesterday."

"Who? Please don't tell me one of my friends came before your grievance committee."

He shook his head. "As if I would tell you about a confidential proceeding, come on, think about it, Quinn, it will come to you."

"Just tell me, Nick, I've had a hard day, I don't want to do any more thinking. My brain is fried."

"I'll give you a hint," he said, "It's a woman."

"Way to narrow it down, Nick. That's only fifty percent of the population."

"She said she used to think your name was *Babe*."

"Jayashree Patel? What is she doing in town?"

Just then, Grace returned with menus, a bag of cheddar popcorn, and a flight of four beer samples ranging in color from light to dark.

"I don't know," Nick said. "But I think there's something big going on."

# Chapter Twenty-Four

"*Of course* it's something big, Nick," I said. "The FBI doesn't come to town to drink mojitos on the beach, you know."

He gave me a look that said he was ready to call that Uber for me.

"Whoa, what did I miss?" Grace asked after setting the beers and popcorn down and distributing the menus.

"Your boyfriend is keeping secrets," I said, taking a swig of the lightest beer. "Hey, that's a good one, dibs!"

"Your best friend is telling lies," Nick said, making a face at me.

"So much drama at this table!" Grace laughed. "If Nick is keeping secrets, Jamie, I'm sure he has his reasons. Like client confidentiality or national security--"

"--Or he wants to keep all the fun cases for himself," I said. "Come on, Nick, tell us why Jayashree is here, she wouldn't mind. You know, I helped her bust that money laundering operation and before that a corrupt commissioner. I mean, I'm practically an FBI consultant."

Nick's face had an odd expression, like he was holding back a sneeze and then he burst out laughing. Grace joined him a few seconds later.

"You--an FBI consultant--that's the funniest...thing...I've ever...heard!" he gasped.

"I told you that you watch too much TV, Jamie," Grace quipped.

Nick wiped his eyes. "Are you Castle or are you Monk?"

"Well," I said, "since they're both off the air, neither. And I'm not Psych or that hot guy from White Collar either. I'll be starting a new series with a *female* consultant. It will be called: *Jamie Quinn, FBI Secret Weapon.*

They both cracked up again and this time I did too.

"You know," Nick said. "I don't watch TV but I'd watch that. I'd even record it so I never missed an episode."

I nodded. "That's because you can totally picture me as an
74

FBI consultant, just admit it. The show would have to be a dramedy, of course. I can't bottle up all this hilarity, it bubbles over."

"Right!" Grace said. "I'm thinking *I Love Lucy* meets *Murder, She Wrote*."

"Now, you're being ridiculous, Gracie," I said. "I look more like Desi Arnaz than Lucille Ball. He was Cuban, right?"

Grace took a sip of the darkest beer in the flight and smacked her lips. "That's funny already--a girl with an Irish name who looks Cuban."

Nick grabbed a handful of popcorn. "Be sure to include the scene where you find a missing key by rolling around in paint with a bunch of rescue dogs."

I threw popcorn at him, but he ducked.

"Hey, that's my dinner, don't waste it," he said.

"Now, Nick," Grace said, "give credit where credit is due. Jamie's technique may be unusual but she does stumble onto clues somehow."

"Yeah, Mr. State Attorney, how about that?" I said, downing the rest of my tiny beer.

He laughed. "Stumble is the operative word, Quinn. Having the Russian mob try to kill you doesn't seem like much of a technique."

"Shows how much you know. At least Grace gets me, right, Bestie?"

"I get you alright," she said. "And when you start calling me Bestie, I know you should eat something before you have another drink. Let's check out the food trucks, shall we?"

"On one condition," I said. "Nick has to answer a question truthfully."

"I always tell the truth, Quinn. When have I ever lied to you?" He leaned back in the booth with that self-righteous air of his.

I thought about it. "How would I know? Besides, a liar would say the same thing."

"Just ask your question already," he said with an eye roll.

"Okay. If you find out what Jayashree is doing here, will you tell me?"

75

"Not a chance."

I shook my head. "You blew it, Nick. When I get my own TV show, I'm making you the villain."

"Can't wait," he said. "Make sure my character is good-looking."

"Yeah, but remember, the bad guy never gets the girl," I said. "That's a fact."

Grace reached over and squeezed his arm. "Yes, but in this case we can make an exception."

# Chapter Twenty-Five

Thanks to Grace and her food intervention, I wasn't too hung over the next morning. I did have a little headache but willed it away with the power of positive thinking--that, and a couple of aspirin. As a result, I was feeling pretty good by the time my neighbors Sandy and Mike called to invite me over for a pizza party. It was their niece Katie's eighth birthday and the first time they would have a house full of sugared-up kids. I interpreted the invitation as a cry for help, a plea for reinforcements, and an acknowledgement that they were in over their heads. While I didn't relish spending my afternoon with a dozen shrieking little girls, I took pity on them and agreed to "drop by".

A few minutes later, I followed my lazy cat out to the patio as I cradled my second cup of coffee. My stomach wasn't up for drinking it but holding the warm cup eased my slight queasiness. As I basked in the sun and counted the number of newly-hatched caterpillars on my milkweed plants, I couldn't help but wonder again why Jayashree Patel was in town. It wasn't like Hollywood, Florida was a hotbed of criminal activity. And despite rumors to the contrary, I never went looking for trouble--it wasn't my fault if I had an inquiring mind. That same inquiring mind urged me to go inside and search the internet for the news about Hollywood and the FBI's most-wanted list. Who knew that the FBI had more than one list of bad guys? Fun fact, their white collar list includes several women who are big-time con artists. Amateurs need not apply.

Feeling a bit apprehensive, I clicked on the next list, the one with the cyber criminals, knowing what I would find: Eugeny Belov, alias Viktor Volodin, was still number one. He was the bastard who had hijacked my computer, tried to kill me and Grace, and murdered Katie's parents. Unfortunately, the FBI still hadn't caught him, but thanks to me they now had his picture. Another victory for *Jamie Quinn, FBI Secret Weapon*. Take that, Nick D.

Aside from Belov, none of the career criminals on any of the FBI lists had a connection to Florida. Did that mean Jayashree had come back for Belov? Could he be looking for me? A shiver ran down my spine. *Hold the phone, Jamie, if Belov was after anyone, it would be Marvin Glasser. Belov only tried to kill you in order to frame Glasser.* Although I would have been just as dead, it was comforting to know it was nothing personal. Anyway, if I were truly in danger, Jayashree would have warned me and that made me feel better. It was funny how I spent so much time talking my clients off the ledge (metaphorically speaking) without realizing I needed to give myself that talk once in a while.

As for news about Hollywood and its environs, I couldn't find anything, which was not surprising. It was the dog days of summer, the tourists were gone and the wealthy people had fled to cooler climes. The only stories of note were about a woman who faked her own kidnapping to test her boyfriend's loyalty and a man who dressed in scrubs so he could steal drugs from the hospital. Welcome to South Florida where novelists can lift plots right from the headlines, no embellishment required.

My cell rang and when I saw whose picture popped up, I answered it. "Speaking of strange people in South Florida, how's it going, Duke? Aren't you up kind of early after your wild night?"

Duke chuckled. "Darlin', what you call a wild night, I call Tuesday. Let me tell ya what a wild night looks like--"

"I'll pass," I said.

"Some other time then," he said. "I'm actually calling to hear more about your conspiracy theory. Are secret agents tailing you or what?"

"If they were, I doubt that I'd know about it," I reasoned, taking a sip of tepid coffee and instantly regretting it.

"Yeah," Duke agreed. "They're pretty lousy spies if you can catch 'em in the act."

"So true, but maybe these guys were disguised as rappers," I teased. "Then they would blend into the crowd."

"You got that right, Ms. Esquire. No conspiracy then?"

"Don't sound so disappointed, Broussard. Hey, how's your investigation going with the forged Chagall?"

"The who?"

"The painting, Duke. You know, the forgery?" I walked

into the kitchen and cracked some eggs into a bowl. Breakfast time at last.

"Why didn't you just say that?" he groused. "Tell you the truth, I'm out of ideas."

"But I'm not," I said, excited. "Do you think Jeff would let you borrow the painting for a few days?"

"Course he would," Duke said. "It's not worth anything."

"Good, because I found an art appraiser who can take a look at it."

Duke paused. "I must've heard you wrong, girl, 'cause there's no way you just said let's take a worthless painting and get an appraisal. Jeff would fire me in a heartbeat! Hell, I'd fire myself."

I clattered dishes as I prepared my food. "Sorry about the noise. You heard me right, I said let's get an appraisal."

Duke sighed. "Does the smart lady lawyer have a reason for doing something so dumb?"

"Yes," I said, "she does."

# Chapter Twenty-Six

"An appraiser determines the value of a painting, right?" I asked.

"Sure," Duke said, "if it's a le-gi-ti-mate painting."

"Exactly!" I flipped my omelet over to cook the other side. "And how does he do that?"

"Beats me, but it's startin' to look like a triple Bloody Mary morning over here..."

I laughed. "Don't blame me for your bad habits, Marmaduke. Did you figure it out yet? Or should I tell you?"

"Wait, don't tell me...to determine the value, he first has to be sure it's the genuine article."

"Right!" I said. "And so..."

"And so he can spot a forged painting. But we already know the picture is a forgery! Just tell me already, I give up," Duke sounded bummed.

"You were so close," I said, splashing Tabasco liberally over my beautiful omelet--speaking of a work of art. "Here's my thinking. A good appraiser will have seen his share of forgeries. Since there are probably a limited number of decent forgers out there, he might--"

"Know who they are!" Duke said triumphantly. "Smart thinkin', Jamie."

"I can't take the credit," I said. "You taught me everything I know."

"Yeah, I did, didn't I?" That was Duke, humble to a fault.

"If you could borrow the painting from Jeff, I'll make the appointment with the appraiser. It might cost around three hundred dollars."

"I'm on it," Duke said. "You coming?"

"I'd love to. If you don't mind..."

"Why would I mind? We're a team," he said.

"Yeah, like Laurel and Hardy, Abbott and Costello..." I said.

"Cheech and Chong..."

80

"Turner and Hooch?" I added.
Duke laughed. "I'll catch ya later, Ms. Esquire."
"Later, Duke."

\*\*\*

After spending an hour planning my upcoming seminar, I ran out to buy a birthday gift for Katie. I didn't want to show up empty-handed, but had no idea what to get her. She was a talented artist with so many art supplies already she could open her own store. She adored Mr. Paws and I would've happily given him to her (with a big bow on his head to annoy him), but Mike and Sandy would have immediately sent him back. Besides, they were thinking of getting her a puppy for Christmas. Maybe I should get a puppy, too--that would *really* annoy Mr. Paws...

The toy store was overwhelming with way too many options, some of them incredibly expensive. The technology available in children's toys was mind-boggling. I read somewhere that a musical birthday card has more computing power than the Allied Forces had in 1945. And we all know what happens to that card post-birthday-- it gets tossed in the trash. Given a little time, those expensive toys would probably wind up in the same landfill.

As I wandered the aisles, I tried to remember what it felt like to be eight. I was never a big fan of Barbie dolls, but I did like puzzles and board games--and books, lots of books. Yes, I was a child nerd, a mini-me of the nerd I was destined to become. I even took a book to a sleepover once, which made me very popular as you might imagine. Okay, not popular, but it did get me shaving cream in my hair. The other thing I liked when I was eight was visiting the antique store. Thinking of Clarence Petersen gave me an idea for the perfect gift for Katie, a gift that never went out of style. A salesperson directed me to the right aisle and soon I was on my way home to wrap the present.

I showed up at my neighbors' house at the same time as the pizza delivery guy, his arms stacked high with boxes. I rang the doorbell for him so he wouldn't drop his precious cargo. We were greeted with squeals of excitement and when Katie gave me a hug,

81

the other girls did too. They were so sweet I wanted to take them all home with me.

Sandy walked over to me looking quite frazzled; her long hair had escaped its neat ponytail and she had pink frosting on her white blouse. She handed me a slice of pizza on a paper plate and wiped her greasy hands on her jeans. Motherhood seemed like a messy undertaking.

"Thanks for coming, Jamie, you're a real trooper!"

I laughed. "Thanks for the invite. It seems like you have everything under control."

"Not at all!" She laughed. "You missed the breaking of the piñata, that was intense. We had to do it outside because I didn't want blindfolded girls swinging a baseball bat in the house. In the end, Mike had to rip the piñata open with his bare hands and the girls almost ran him over diving for candy. Jamie, you didn't have to bring a present."

Taking a bite of pizza, I said "Of course I did, Katie's my buddy."

"Well, what is it?" She shook the large rectangular box.

"You'll have to wait and see, but I promise it's not noisy and there's no assembly required."

"Give me another hint," she said.

"Let's just say everyone needs a little magic in their lives."

# Chapter Twenty-Seven

Sunday was errand day and I couldn't have been less enthusiastic. If only Katie's new magic wand could make my chores disappear. Snuggled up cozy under my quilt, I would've happily stayed there all day but eventually had to drag myself out of bed. I was a reluctant housekeeper on my best day and kept hoping someone would invent a self-cleaning house--like a self-cleaning cat, minus the attitude. Until then, not only did I have to dust, vacuum, take out the trash, do the laundry, shop for groceries and pay the bills, I also had to schlep to my office to make copies for La Vida Boca. Whose dumb idea was that again? Oh yeah, mine. The only bright spot in my day would be my weekly Skype call with my dad in Nicaragua. I decided to call from the office while the copy machine was doing its thing.

I always started my cleaning by dusting and vacuuming, to work up some momentum before tackling the bathrooms. The rhythmic back and forth of vacuuming coupled with the white noise of the motor allowed my mind wander free as the dust motes floating in the air. After vanquishing the tumbleweeds of cat hair with my mighty Dyson, I rested for a minute. I knew I'd only won the battle, not the war, and soon a new army of tumbleweeds would lay siege to my house. If my vacuum cleaner ever broke I'd just have to move.

Sundays didn't use to be such a drag. Before Kip took off to save the wombats, we had fun running around town. We would go to the Yellow Green Farmers' Market to buy fresh produce and wolf down free samples of chocolate chip banana bread, Amish cheese, Greek olives, and local honey. We would play with the puppies at the dog rescue booth and once, we even danced to the Jimmy Buffett cover band playing near the picnic tables. Afterwards, we usually stopped at a Broward park so Kip could check on something for work, like how the Scottish Festival was going or whether the baby turtles had hatched overnight. I never knew what to expect. One thing I loved about Kip was his endless curiosity--whether it was a bug, an app, or a new theory of time travel, he always found it fascinating. He could take it too far though. I didn't mind if he wanted to check out a cool bug, but after ten minutes of that I'd have to drag him away. I'm sure all couples had the same arrangement.

If it sounds like I'd put my life on hold when Kip left, I can't deny it. I can't explain it either. It seemed like all I ever did anymore was wait around--wait for my dad, wait for Kip--and now I was waiting for both of them. It wasn't like the Yellow Green Farmers' Market had a poster with my picture on it and the caption *Keep out, Jamie (you eat too many free samples)*. I could've gone there anytime I wanted, but I never did. Well, I was through waiting. First order of business would be to plan my trip to Nicaragua (again). If Kip happened to come home while I was gone, then he could wait for me for a change. Who was in favor of taking charge of her own life? Show of hands, please. It's unanimous, the resolution has passed.

***

I parked my Mini Cooper in the empty lot behind my office and unlocked the mailbox to collect Saturday's mail. Pleadings and correspondence came by e-mail now and snail mail had become fairly sparse. My bills were also paid online which left only checks and advertisements to fill the box. In a good month I received more checks than junk mail. I skimmed the stack and saw that most of the mail was for Nelda so I decided to sort it later. Yes, it's true, Nelda's clients hogged the mailbox the same way they hogged the waiting room.

I punched in the alarm code, suppressing my usual panic that my brain had somehow lost the sequence and that shrieking alarms would summon a SWAT team in short order. I wasn't just being paranoid because: a) I'd set off the alarm before, and b) I was that girl in school who always forgot her locker combination after winter break. If this were the movie *Memento*, I would have tattooed the critical information on my arms like the protagonist did. Now, there was a guy who understood his shortcomings and compensated

84

accordingly.

The office was peaceful on the weekend, no ringing phones, no crabby clients, no noise at all. But that wasn't enough reason to visit; my house was quiet too, and had better snacks. After turning on the lights, the computer, and the copy machine, I set up my packet to copy and collate. It was already one o'clock, which was eleven a.m. in Managua, and my dad would be expecting my call. I stopped in the bathroom to make sure my hair wasn't sticking up (any more than usual) and that I didn't have food in my teeth. I was ready to Skype.

"Hola Papi!" I said when he materialized, curly white hair and plentiful eyebrows framing his weathered, pleasant face. His olive skin looked more tanned than usual, but there was something else different, something I couldn't put my finger on.

"Ah, Jamie! How wonderful to see you, mi hija."

He beamed at me from the laptop that I'd bought him. The connection was so crisp he might have been sitting across the table from me. I felt like I could reach over and touch his hand, yet my mind knew he was a thousand miles away. We had grown so close over our many months of Skype calls that our relationship felt genuine and solid. It was hard to believe we'd never met in person, never been in the same room. Using Skype had allowed me to watch myself star in my own live action film as I spoke with my dad. Seeing the two of us juxtaposed on split screens was like looking in a mirror, or through a window into my future. We were so alike in our expressions, our mannerisms, our curly, frizzy hair, how we laughed, our love of sci-fi. We even hated the same foods--all of that it had to be genetic, there was no other explanation. As soon as I could isolate that gene for sci-fi geekiness that we shared, I'd be rich. Until then, I would have to keep showing up for work.

"I have a surprise for you," I announced.

"And I have a surprise for you," he said with a deep belly laugh.

"You go first," I said.

"Are you sure?" he teased.

I realized then what was different about my father. He looked happier, more relaxed, even the pinch between his eyebrows had vanished.

"I'm positive. Tell me, Papi, what's your surprise?"

"I'm glad you're sitting down because this is big, big news. I finished my studies and got my degree! It took over thirty-five years, but I finally did it. Por fin!"

I squealed with excitement. "Wow, that's incredible! I'm so proud of you! Why didn't you tell me you were doing that? What's your degree in?"

His brown eyes were shining with emotion. "To hear my daughter say she is proud of me is all I could ever ask." He sniffed and wiped his eyes. "To answer your question, my degree is in agriculture. It's from UNAN, la Universidad Nacional Autónoma de Nicaragua."

I smiled fondly at him through my webcam. "Ana Maria must be so thrilled about this. I'm sorry I missed your graduation, but I'll make it up to you. Do you want to hear my surprise now?"

"Of course I do!" He wagged his finger at me for doubting him.

"I'm coming to visit you, Papi!"

This is where things got strange. Instead of expressing the joyful exuberance I expected, my dad looked like a deflated balloon.

"Um...is that a problem?" I stammered. "I mean...I didn't buy the ticket yet--"

"No, no," he said, trying to recover his composure. "*Of course* I would love to see you, Jamie, it's just that...things aren't...how do you say it, *settled* right now. My job has me traveling around, you know?"

I didn't say anything for a few seconds. I could tell he was lying but I had no idea why. One thing about Skype--it made it harder to lie, but I had an advantage from years of dealing with clients; I had an excellent poker face.

"Oh, okay. I thought the job was over with," I said, keeping my voice neutral. "I must have gotten that wrong. You let me know when it's a good time, okay?"

His relief was almost palpable as he gave me a broad smile. "Nothing would make me happier than to see my beautiful daughter at last! I can't wait until that day comes."

I could tell he meant it. What was going on here? Maybe I could corner Ana Maria and get some answers. So much for me taking charge of my life.

After we said our good-byes, I sat in front of the dark computer screen lost in thought. How had my dad managed to make me feel so loved and so rejected all in a span of fifteen minutes? I was on an emotional roller coaster that I didn't remember buying a ticket for. Here he had the chance to meet his only child, the one he didn't even know he had, and he blew it. The men in my life were stressing me out and I wished I knew what to do about it.

The copy machine was done and I was more than ready to leave, but I still had to sort the mail. Aside from a Bar Journal and some flyers, there was only one letter addressed to me. It was thick, with a local postmark and no return address, so it wasn't from a law office, it wasn't a check, and it wasn't a bar complaint--those envelopes were thick, with the return address of The Florida Bar and the power to induce heart palpitations. I ripped the envelope open and examined the strange contents.

"What the hell is this?" I said out loud.

But nobody answered me.

.

# Chapter Twenty-Eight

I couldn't make sense of the packet in my hand. It was an amalgamation of a lawsuit, a letter, and a contract titled *Invoice Billing for Copyright Infringement, per Contract.* Underneath that it read: Issued by Marcus Joseph, family of Wise, sovereign.

*Sovereign?* Who was Marcus Joseph Wise?

The first paragraph stated that the invoice was issued in regards to the unauthorized use of a duly recorded copyright, MARCUS J. WISE ©.

The next paragraph was titled: DEMAND FOR PAYMENT and contained loads of legal gobbledygook and an accusation that I, Jamie Quinn, had made unauthorized use of his duly recorded copyright MARCUS J. WISE © and, as a result, he was entitled to damages per contract.

*We had a contract?*

The next section laid out the damages, a paltry $1.5 million dollars, due within thirty days. Failure to pay within that time would lead to a ten percent penalty being added. Also, my account with him was *overdrawn and now closed.* My failure to pay would result in him issuing a criminal complaint for copyright infringement AND unjust enrichment.

*I was unjustly enriched?*

The second page (oh, yes, there was more) was even crazier, starting with the title: Truth Affidavit in the Nature of Supplemental Rules for Maritime Claims.

*Apparently, we were now under Maritime Law. This guy was definitely lost at sea.*

More gobbledygook and then this paragraph: **I, Me, My, Myself,** MARCUS J. WISE, the undersigned for We the People, Sovereigns, natural born living souls, the Posterity, born upon the land in the several States united for America, *(blah blah blah)* do hereby solemnly declare, say and state: I am competent for stating the matters set forth herewith.

*He was competent?! I would've lost that bet.*

There was so much more, but I'll cut to what seemed to be

88

the essence of his complaint, chock full of juicy craziness:

**Fact:** The person known as MARCUS J. WISE is fiction without form or substance, *(was he a ghost?)* for We the People of Florida from our Life, Liberty, Property, and Pursuit of Happiness, for their self-enrichment outside the law authority and our Courts by original jurisdiction.

*Oh, boy! This guy's favorite dish was word salad.*

I felt like I was back in college reading Chaucer in Old English. The words almost made sense, but in the end, they just gave me a headache. I had no idea who Marcus J. Wise was or when I'd had the audacity to misappropriate his name, but I did know one thing. I couldn't wait to violate his "copyright" again and show this masterpiece to Grace. It was worth racking up another 1.5 million dollars in 'damages' to see her face. Who knew practicing law could be so entertaining?

After locking up the office, I set the alarm without incident and called Grace from the car to see if I could stop by on my way home. When she answered, I thought I'd dialed the wrong number, which was impossible since her number was programmed into my phone.

"Gracie? You sound awful! What's going on?"

"Ah, hey James, I'm sick as a dog, that's what. My nose is a toxic waste site and I think I just coughed up a lung. Other than that, I'm peachy."

"Well, thanks for sharing! What can I do for you, my friend? Do you want some soup? Medicine? A case of Kleenex?"

"You're sweet, but I just have to tough it out. I wish I knew who gave me this cold so I could punch them in the face." She blew her nose loudly in my ear.

"I can take care of that for you, no problem," I said. "One question--what if the cold killed 'patient zero'? I can't punch them if they're dead."

"Just find their next of kin and punch them instead," she said with a hoarse laugh that morphed into a hacking cough.

"Seems a bit extreme," I said, "but I'll do it for you. I kinda hope it's Nick though. He's overdue for a punch."

# Chapter Twenty-Nine

It was Monday morning and already a scorcher with heat shimmering off the asphalt in waves. Just walking from my car to the entrance of La Vida Boca made me sweat so much my make-up started to melt. Terrific, first day on the job and I looked like a reject from Madame Tussaud's wax museum. *Way to make a good impression, Jamie.*

As the automatic doors whooshed open, a blast of cold air greeted me like an old friend and I stopped in the foyer to catch my breath. This was my third visit to the assisted living facility (ALF for short, not to be confused with 'Alien Life Form') and the lobby looked the same as it had the first time. Nobody had moved since then, or so it seemed. The same elderly people were parked next to the same walkers, wheelchairs, and oxygen tanks, in the same spots, wearing the same bulky sweaters. Wait a minute--sweaters? I was fainting from heat prostration and they were dressed for light snow flurries. Unreal.

Dazed from the heat, I scanned the room trying to figure out where my seminar would be held. I glanced at Wilma's picture on the wall hoping for some guidance but it had nothing to say on the matter. That left Glenda, guardian of the front desk, who disliked interruptions, especially from me, to tell me where to go. I got the impression she'd like to tell everyone where to go. I was heading her way when I ran into someone I had met on my first visit.

"Hello, Herb!" I said, "Fancy meeting you here."

Herb Lowenthal shook his head with his usual enthusiasm. "Where else am I going to be, Jamie Quinn, at a Broadway Show? Maybe out dancing? Are you here for the seminar?"

"No, I'm not here for the seminar," I said matter-of-factly. "I *am* the seminar." Herb smiled at that. "Do you know where I'm supposed to be?"

"I know everything. Stick with me, kid, and you can't go wrong."

Herb's bushy eyebrows were more active today but his two

90

tufts of hair looked like soft clouds had touched down above his ears and might fly away at any moment. As I followed my guide down the main corridor, we walked past the Bingo hall before stopping in the next room, which held a conference table with ten chairs and smelled of antiseptic. The only indication that this was the right place was the box of pens on the table. Then again, maybe those pens were always there. We were the only occupants.

I turned to Herb. "I know I'm early, but..."

"They'll be here, don't worry," he said, making his caterpillar eyebrows dance. They just don't move so fast. Believe me, your seminar is the highlight of their day."

"Surely, there's something better to watch on TV," I joked. "Like *The People's Court* or *Judge Judy*."

"Nah," he said, "they get tired of yelling at the TV after a while."

I didn't know what to say to that so I started unpacking my briefcase. An eternal optimist, I'd brought fifty sets of forms with me, but only took out ten. Then I pulled out the paper plates, napkins and fruit salad I'd bought that morning and arranged them artfully on the table.

"You brought food? What kind of lawyer serves food?" Herb asked, surprised.

I smiled. "I figure if this law stuff doesn't work out, I can always go into catering."

"Makes sense," Herb said. He took a plate and started helping himself. "Don't mind if I do."

"Oh, good," I said, "does that mean you're staying? I could use the moral support."

"I wouldn't miss it," he said stabbing at a piece of pineapple with his plastic fork. After two tries, he scooped it up with his hand and popped it in his mouth. "Besides, I have to point out the loonies for you." He circled his finger near his head in the universal gesture for crazy. "In lawyer-speak, they're non compos mentis."

"I was told nobody like that was coming," I said, annoyed. "I can't be responsible for--"

"Not to worry," Herb said with a shrug. "There are all kinds of crazies in this world, am I right?"

91

"You're not making me feel better, you know." I chided him.

While we waited, I wondered if Herb was going to leave any fruit for the rest of the group. I tried to make small talk.

"So, what's your story, Herb? You seem like an interesting guy."

Without missing a beat, he said: "Why, you writing a book? How about you make it a mystery and leave my chapter out."

Unfazed, I replied: "But my book is about this cool guy who saves the day--and I was planning to name him Herb."

With a gravelly laugh, he pointed his plastic fork at me. "You've got moxie, Jamie Quinn, I like that. You're fast on your feet, too." He gave me a shrewd, appraising look which included some eyebrow action. "Okay, you're hired."

"Hired to do what?" I asked, but I didn't have the chance to find out because my students had arrived en masse, all four of them. Herb's warning notwithstanding, they looked competent to me. The three women and lone man were all neatly dressed, well-groomed, and wearing sensible shoes. Naturally.

I gave them a welcoming smile. "Good morning, my name is--"

"Hey, where's that handsome fellow who's usually here?" One of the women interrupted. "The one who looks like Alex Trebek. Where's Miles?"

Before I could respond, the woman in the beige pantsuit and tortoise shell glasses answered for me. "Miles left, Tillie, don't you remember? He moved to Costa Rica with his husband."

"His what?" the third woman asked, confusion all over her face.

"Now, girls, don't y'all be rude to our guest," said the tall man with a lion's mane of white hair and a Carolina accent. He took my hand in a faux-handshake which was more of a squeeze. "This here is our new lawyer lady. She's quite the improvement over Miles, if you ask me."

"And who asked you, Mr. Casanova?" Herb said.

Mr. Casanova laughed. "I don't need to be asked. Charming the ladies is what I do." He tipped an imaginary hat in my direction and I suddenly realized who he reminded me of.

"Pleased to meet ya, ma'am. My name is Lucas Merriweather Jones but all my friends call me--"

"--Luke?" I interjected gleefully. I couldn't believe it--this guy was Duke in about thirty years--and *still* hitting on women.

"Maybe his friends call him that," Herb said with a dismissive wave, "but the rest of us call him Mr. Casanova. There's no fool like an old fool, am I right?"

At that moment, Jodi Martin's strawberry blonde head appeared in the doorway. "Hey Jamie, can you come see me when you're done?"

"Sure," I said. "In the garden?"

She gave me a nod and then she was gone. I hoped she had news for me since I didn't have any for her. I turned to my 'students' who were munching on fruit and arguing about something or other. It dawned on me that I wasn't teaching a seminar, I was herding cats. Time to call this class to order. Reaching into my briefcase (my bag of tricks) I pulled out a recent purchase, the silver bell with the Pegasus on top, and rang it loudly in case anyone had a hearing issue. (I also had a whistle to keep people in line at mediation. It was kind of a joke, but I did have to use it one time when things got nasty.)

Once I had everyone's attention, I said "Let's get started, shall we? My name is Jamie Quinn and I'm here today to explain this packet of forms--"

"This fruit is delicious!" Tillie said. "Where did you get it, if you don't my asking?"

"Well, I'm glad you like it. I--"

"Oh, for Pete's sake!" Herb said. "It's a fruit salad. Don't act like you've never had fruit salad before. What are you, from Mars? Let her talk."

If Tillie's feelings were hurt, it was hard to tell as she'd gone back to eating.

"The first page," I said, "is a *Durable Family Power of Attorney*. This form allows you to appoint a family member to act on your behalf by signing legal documents, transferring property, etc. The benefit of having this is--"

93

"I'm sorry to interrupt," said the woman in the beige pantsuit, her tortoise shell glasses reflecting the fluorescent lights, "but you don't need to--"

A sharp knock on the doorframe made us jump. It was Wilma and she was dressed in a lime pantsuit that clashed terribly with her dyed red bouffant. If it was attention she was after, that was one way to get it.

"How are we doing this morning?" she chirped. "Everyone pay attention today to learn about these important legal documents." Then she gave us a phony smile, clapped her hands to make sure everyone was awake, twirled on her heel and left.

"Okay, where were we? You were saying something?" I said to the nice beige lady.

She nodded and smiled. "Yes, I was saying that you don't need to explain these forms to us."

"Why not?" I asked.

"Because we already signed them a long time ago."

# Chapter Thirty

"Huh?" was all I could manage, proving I wasn't as fast on my feet as Herb imagined. "Is that true?"

Herb shrugged and the rest of them nodded. Tillie was busy eating, using my forms packet as a placemat.

"Then why did you come today?" I asked them. "Was there a misunderstanding? If so, I'm sorry I wasted your time."

Luke flashed a dazzling smile and I could see why he was such a hit with the ladies. "Waste of time? This is the most fun I've had all week. Now that we broke the ice and all, want to hear a joke?" He drummed his long fingers on the table in anticipation.

I was skeptical. "Is it rated G, as in safe for grandmas?"

"Not on your life." He grinned.

"Then the answer is no, Duke--I mean, *Luke*." I grabbed a handful of grapes from the bowl and ate one. "Let's start over. If you already signed these forms, what did Miles talk about when he came?"

Tillie beamed. "Oh, Miles was wonderful! He told us funny stories and made us laugh and laugh. Such a handsome man, too!"

"Yeah, you mentioned that," I said. "Did the other residents ever come to the seminars?"

"Eh, once in a while," Herb said.

"What you're saying is that this isn't a seminar at all, it's more like a koffee klatch or an open mike night for Luke?"

"Yep, you nailed it." Luke said. He had pulled a deck of cards from his pocket and was doing tricks for Tillie's amusement.

I stood up. "This isn't right, I'm getting paid to teach a seminar, not goof around. Does Wilma know about this?" I directed my question to Herb.

"Relax, my young friend, she knows, of course she knows." Herb paused and took his phone out of his pocket to check on something (yet he still liked to read an old-fashioned newspaper; some habits die hard). He went on, "Believe me, if Wilma wanted people here she would have combined it with Bingo. It's not your problem, Jamie Quinn. You just show up and if they come, they come. As a side note, I admire your integrity. You sure you're a lawyer?"

I sat down again. "I don't know if that's a compliment or an insult, Herb."

He laughed. "My brother Myron was a lawyer, but I didn't hold it against him either. Look at it this way, you're like an insurance policy, you're there if we need you. Feel better now?"

I shook my head. "I'll get back to you on that." I pulled my packet apart using my nails to loosen the staple and held up the three forms. "Are you all positive that you filled out *these* forms?"

Everyone nodded, even Tillie who didn't know what she was agreeing to and who was still clearly pining for Miles.

"Okay then, class dismissed. See you next month, I guess. Bring your friends!"

Luke tipped his imaginary hat on his way out and Tillie took the tray of fruit with her. Only Herb stayed behind.

"You could've warned me," I scolded him.

"True," he said with an unconcerned nod. "What, are you waiting for an apology?"

"Maybe." I began wiping the sticky table with a wet napkin.

"You know, lawyers are supposed to be tough," he joked.

"And old people are supposed to be nice and hand out peppermint candies."

At that Herb laughed so much the map of wrinkles on his face rearranged themselves into a new country entirely. "You're a kick in the pants, Jamie Quinn! You remind me of my daughter. She was funny and smart too, and talented, oy, was she talented...." His mood had shifted like the wind.

"Herb," I said from my heart, "I'm honored to be compared to your daughter." Poor man, no wonder he didn't want to talk about himself.

Herb studied his arthritic hands resting on the table. He finally spoke. "It was drugs that killed her, but she fell in with some very bad people. I blame them."

I wanted to comfort him, but all I could say was I'm sorry and all I could do was keep him company. So, that's what I did. We sat together a little while before being interrupted in the best way

96

possible. Our favorite chocolate Labradoodle, Marley, trotted in like he owned the place, which he must've thought he did since he was there so often. I forgot that Jessie came every week to do pet therapy--I mean, I knew, but somehow it had slipped my mind. What can I say? A lot had happened since the previous Monday and my head could only hold so much information. I don't know what my brain was so busy doing besides bombarding me with annoying commercials at three a.m.; it was never there when I needed it. I'd be lucky if I remembered where I parked my car.

Marley lay on the floor, hoping for a belly rub. Herb had cheered up and all he needed were some wet, sloppy dog kisses. Pet therapy really worked.

Herb stood up to leave. "Well then, it's decided. You're hired, Jamie Quinn. You passed your job interview with flying colors."

"But--" I trailed off.

"But, what?" Herb asked, as if this were a normal way to enter a business relationship.

"I won't be your hired gun," was all I could think of to say.

"Of course not," he said and shook my hand firmly to seal the deal, a deal I knew nothing about. "Anything else you won't do?"

I thought about it. "I don't do windows," I joked.

He nodded. "Me, either."

"Because you don't have to?" I said.

"No, because I own a Mac. Bye, Jamie Quinn, see you soon."

# Chapter Thirty-One

"What was that all about?" Jessie asked. She had walked in while I was talking to Herb.

"No idea," I said.

"Yeah, Herb is like that, very mysterious. How was your seminar?" She dropped into a chair and started scratching behind Marley's ears causing his tail to wag like a windshield wiper on a rainy day. They clearly had an understanding.

"It was a disaster. Or a success--depends on who you ask."

I polished off my last two grapes wishing Tillie had left me a few more. It hurt to be outsmarted by a senior citizen with a shaky grip on reality. You snooze, you lose, that's the rule.

"Sorry I didn't get back to you," Jess said, tucking a strand of wavy purple-tinged hair behind her ear. "We had a minor crisis at the shelter and I didn't have a chance to call Uncle Teddy. How did you wind up at Clarence Petersen's memorial anyway?"

"Bad timing. It turns out I actually knew Clarence back when I was a kid. Isn't that strange?" I reached over to pet Marley's shaggy head.

Jessie smiled. "Sounds like an episode of *The Twilight Zone* to me. Hey, I want to find out what Shirley Petersen was ranting about. Let's go ask Uncle Teddy. Come on!"

With that, she sprung up from her chair and was out the door before I could finish saying okay. Instead of turning toward the lobby, Jessie and Marley headed left down a long serpentine corridor as I valiantly tried to keep up. We were walking at such a fast clip I couldn't look down at the carpet because the pattern was making me dizzy--weren't old folks' homes supposed to be soothing? Jessie zipped past the residents like she was in a movie set on fast-forward and they were on freeze-frame. We finally stopped when we reached the stairwell.

"Whoa! Where-are-we-go-ing?" I protested, catching my breath. "Is your uncle locked in a tower or something? Why didn't we just take the elevator in the lobby?"

Jessie burst into giggles. "Oh, sorry, I was imagining Uncle

Teddy locked in a tower! Too funny. We couldn't go through the lobby because everyone would've wanted to play with Marley. My uncle's place is three flights up, can you make it?"

"What am I, eighty? *Of course* I can make it." I said, slightly winded and mildly offended. I kicked off my pumps and tucked them into the wide pockets of my jacket.

"If Uncle Teddy can do it, I'm sure you can too," Jess assured me before prancing up the stairs on her nimble little feet. Marley wasn't nearly as graceful but he got the job done. I'd never seen a dog climb stairs before; he looked like a small galloping horse.

I made it to the fourth floor, pride intact, and followed Jessie to her uncle's apartment. She called him first to say we were there before letting herself in with her key.

"He's not feeling great today, so he's taking it easy," she whispered as we stepped inside.

We found ourselves in a homey living room with an L-shaped brown leather sofa pushed against the wall, a coffee table centered over a small accent rug in front of it, and reproductions of art on the walls. At least, I assumed they were reproductions. Uncle Teddy, clad only in a worn terrycloth robe cinched over old-fashioned striped pajamas, was sprawled in a Lazy-Boy recliner, left leg propped on an ottoman, a bowl of soup cooling on a snack table by his elbow. He still resembled the Monopoly guy but looked a lot less perky--more likely to send you to jail than to take a ride on the Reading. Even his moustache was droopy.

"How's my favorite uncle?" Jess asked, leaning over to kiss his unshaven cheek.

"I don't know, but when I see him I'll ask him," he said playfully.

Not to be outdone, Marley plunked his front paws in Teddy's lap and panted dog-breath in his face, demanding to be noticed. Teddy fussed over Marley until he was fully satisfied that yes, he *was* a good boy. Seeing all the attention Marley got made me wonder what I was doing wrong. If this was a dog's life, it didn't look so bad.

"Is your gout acting up?" Jessie asked, pointing at her uncle's leg. We were sitting on the sofa facing him.

99

He nodded. "I wouldn't mind it except my damn ulcer flared up at the same time. Getting' old ain't for sissies, that's for sure."

"Yeah, it must be hard," Jessie sympathized.

Her uncle made a face. "Getting old isn't hard, you just have to keep waking up every day. *Being* old is the hard part."

"Okay, Grumpy," Jess said, rising from the sofa. "I'm sure Snow White will be here soon with the other dwarves. In the meantime, do you want some tea?"

Uncle Teddy laughed. "She's a hoot, isn't she?" He looked to me for confirmation before adding, "A cup of tea would be terrific."

As I studied the décor, I recognized a Picasso print of a mother and child and, next to it, a surreal landscape that might've been a Dalí. One art history class in college had made more of an impression on me than three years of law school. What can I say? I liked melting clocks.

"Love the artwork," I said.

"Me too," Teddy admitted grudgingly, "but I didn't used to."

Jessie set the steaming cup on the snack table and we exchanged a look.

"Why did you buy them then?" she asked. "Did they come with the apartment or something?"

Her uncle held up a finger for us to wait while he sipped his tea. How he avoided dunking his long moustache in the cup was a mystery. The only thing better for storing food would have been a beard--or Tupperware. I didn't understand the appeal of growing facial hair, but then again, I couldn't manage the hair on my head.

"Ah," he said, "That hits the spot! Girls, there are two words that guarantee a happy marriage and they are *Yes, dear.* My late wife liked art, so we bought art. She used to drag me to museums and art shows all over the world and I used to say she was cultured like a pearl. That was our little joke."

"Good one!" Jess exclaimed. Seeing my puzzled look she said, "Her name was Pearl."

"Aw, that's sweet," I said.

100

Uncle Teddy gulped the rest of his tea. "The funny thing is," he said, patting his moustache with a napkin, "as I grew older, I started seeing things in a different way. I found meaning in the art that wasn't there before. When I shared that with Pearl, she was really touched, so I let her think it was her doing. Who knows?" he shrugged. "Maybe it was."

"Do you have a favorite?" I asked.

He chuckled. "Now you sound like my wife. Nah, if it speaks to me, I like it. If it makes me feel something or makes me think--which doesn't happen often--that's really something."

Just then the doorbell rang and Jessie got up to answer it. It was Harry, Uncle Teddy's poker buddy, the one who had warned me about the food. He was wearing a different pair of loud pants, but his fashion preference was undeniable. He was mad for plaid.

"Heard you were laid up," he greeted Teddy with a slap on the shoulder. "I had to make sure you were still kicking."

"Well, I won't be joining the Rockettes any time soon," Teddy joked, pointing at his leg, "but I'm still here."

"Then you're still in the running," Harry said, taking a seat next to us on the sofa.

"You bet I am." Uncle Teddy gave him an enthusiastic thumbs up.

Jessie shook her head. "What are you two competing for? Sexiest senior citizen?"

The two men started laughing so hard I was afraid they'd need CPR--which was not in my skillset, unless watching ER counts as training. I was only a *juris* doctor. Law school had prepared me for crises like nasty opponents and crying clients, but nothing life or death. Anyone waiting for me to come to the rescue is out of luck.

When Harry finally caught his breath, he said, "We're trying for world's oldest poker player. The record is currently held by a ninety-six year old."

Teddy shook his head. "The record might stand, but I doubt that the guy is still standing. It's been a few years. Let's just say he probably won't mind when we take his title away."

"Yup, he's way past caring, no doubt about it," Harry agreed, adjusting the sofa pillows so he could sit back. "Poor

Clarence, now he's out of the running. I think the competition was even his idea."

Teddy sniffed and wiped his eyes. "Yeah, I can't believe he's gone. We were friends for forty years, isn't that something?"

*Finally*, we were talking about Clarence. "How did you two meet?" I asked, leaning forward.

Excited, Jessie leaned forward at the same time and accidentally elbowed me in the side.

"Oops, sorry!" she said, suppressing a giggle.

"No problem," I said. "It's only my ribs. I have more, you know, *spare* ribs."

Jess elbowed me again, this time on purpose. "Tell us the story, Uncle Teddy."

Harry chimed in with "I don't think I've heard this one."

Teddy cleared his throat. "I'll start by saying that first impressions aren't worth a hill of beans."

"Why do you think that?" Jessie said.

"Because when I first met Clarence I couldn't stand him."

# Chapter Thirty-Two

"I'll never forget it," Teddy said. "It was St. Patrick's Day, 1976, and I got roped into playing in a charity golf tournament in Miami. Our team was short a man and somehow we ended up with Clarence as our fourth."

"That sounds like fun," Jess said. "You love golf."

"I didn't love it that day," her uncle said wryly.

"What happened?" Harry asked. "Did Clarence run over your foot with the cart, or what?"

"I'm trying to tell a story here," Teddy said with mock exasperation. "You need to know the context. Work with me, people. When you watch a movie, do you skip straight to the end? If so, here are some endings for you: Rosebud is a sled, soylent green is people and King Kong plunges to his death off the Empire State Building."

"Fine, fine," Harry sat back on the sofa and crossed his arms. "Tell your story, you old geezer."

"Thank-you," Teddy said, "I will." He adjusted his leg on the footstool, wincing a little, before continuing. "The day started out bad and went downhill from there. To begin with, the tournament wasn't well-organized, the caddies didn't know where to go, there weren't enough golf carts, and we had to wait for other teams to play through. Then, at the second hole, it started raining-- not enough to cancel the tournament, mind you, just enough to make us miserable. The clubs were slippery and the ground was muddy and Clarence was driving me bonkers. He wouldn't stop telling jokes and giving us tips on how to play."

"Was he a good golfer?" I asked.

"Oh, he was excellent, a genius at reading the green, even in the rain."

"He must have done *something* to make you like him," Jessie remarked.

"Yes, indeed," Uncle Teddy said. "He did two things. First, he choked on the eighteenth hole."

"On purpose?" I guessed.

"Yup," Teddy nodded. "He didn't want us to feel bad. I could see what he was doing and I thought to myself *that's a helluva guy!*"

"What was the second thing?" Harry asked.

"Drinks were on him the rest of the afternoon!" Teddy laughed. "We were fast friends after that and he helped me improve my golf game like you wouldn't believe. I remember us celebrating my first hole-in-one--which was also my last hole-in-one, in case you were wondering. Clarence and I had some really good times together."

Nobody said anything for a few minutes. I wanted to bring up Shirley's behavior at the memorial without seeming like an insensitive clod, but I didn't know how. Then Jessie came right out and asked. Go, Jess!

"Uncle Teddy," she said gently, "was Clarence acting differently these past few months?"

Teddy gazed out the window, Harry looked down at the floor and I avoided eye contact with Jessie so we wouldn't look like the co-conspirators we were. Since we were all looking elsewhere, I tried to read the room, but I couldn't. Maybe the men were uncomfortable talking about their friend's problems, or maybe they felt guilty for not doing more to help.

Jessie broke the silence a second time. "I'm sorry if I upset you, I didn't mean to."

Her uncle shook his head. "It's alright, don't apologize. It's just that it really rattled us to lose Clarence and then to have Shirley accuse us like that..."

"Accuse you?" I blurted out. "Of betraying your friend?"

"Why would you think she was talking about you?" Jess asked, confused.

Harry shrugged. "Who else could it be? Clarence wasn't close to anyone at La Vida Boca except us."

"There's no way she meant you," Jess insisted. "What about Clarence--did he tell you someone had betrayed him?"

"No," Teddy said. "But he was clearly upset about something and he said some things that were off the wall. Right, Harry?"

104

"Oh, yeah! About a month ago, we were all sitting around the pool and out of nowhere he says what if I told you I'm not the person you think I am? I thought he was joking, but he wasn't."

Teddy nodded. "He said something even stranger to me. A few weeks ago, he told me he was going to divorce Shirley for financial reasons. I said what the hell are you talking about, Clarence? He said he had to do it to protect her, but he wouldn't elaborate. Of course, we know he didn't go through with that."

I saw Jessie's expression change, her mouth forming the letter 'O' as she made the connection between me and the Petersens. She understood now why I'd come to see them and she glared at me like I'd been holding out on her, which was true, but I didn't have a choice. I had taken an oath to maintain the confidence and preserve inviolate the secrets of my clients. Although the Petersens weren't technically my clients, the conversation I'd had with Clarence on the phone was a consultation and therefore protected by attorney-client privilege. Only one person had the right to waive that privilege and it was Clarence. Absent a Ouija board, I didn't see that happening.

"Have you tried talking to Shirley?" I asked Teddy in an effort to stop Jessie from revealing what she knew.

Both men looked alarmed at the prospect of approaching the widow and I can't say I blamed them, Shirley *was* kind of scary. Jess immediately came to her uncle's rescue.

"Let me handle this, Uncle Teddy. I'll get to the bottom of it and clear up any misunderstandings. *I'm sure Jamie would love to help me.*"

She used her brown eyes to do a Jedi mind trick that had me nodding my head in agreement. She was a sweet girl, but when it came to her uncle's well-being Jessie took no prisoners. She wouldn't have any trouble speaking to Shirley because she was a little scary herself.

The two men looked relieved and thanked us for our offer (well, Jessie's offer), and agreed it was worth a try. Marley, who had been lying quietly by Teddy's feet, suddenly got up and walked to the door where he stood patiently, waiting for us to notice. It was time to go, but we had what we came for, which was more information.

As Jessie locked the door from the outside, we heard Harry say, "Are you up for the game tonight?"

Teddy laughed. "Of course! How can I be the world's oldest poker player if I don't play poker?"

"Relax," Harry said, "if it doesn't work out, you can settle for world's oldest Parcheesi player."

# Chapter Thirty-Three

"What's with all the secrets?" Jessie demanded once we were in the hallway. "Clarence is gone, you know. He won't mind."

"I took a solemn oath," I said as we walked towards the elevator.

"It doesn't matter. I already know why you were meeting with the Petersens, Miss Jamie Quinn."

I laughed. "I can neither confirm nor deny the allegations. What's more, I plead the Fifth, just because I can."

The empty elevator arrived and we hopped on, Marley between us. I reached over to pet him and he licked my hand.

"What's your plan for talking to Shirley?" I asked. "I don't recommend the direct approach; she seems like one angry octogenarian."

Jessie had an answer ready. "Oh, you mean the plan we're going to carry out together? That plan? You'll love this! We're going to deliver a condolence card from my Uncle Teddy along with a nice plant."

"That's the plan? Sounds pretty lame. You think handing her a plant will make her invite us in for tea and cookies?"

Jessie did a facepalm. "Sheesh, Jamie, it's not a social call. We want to see her reaction."

"To what? A plant?"

"You're getting warmer," she said. "Think about it, what's special about the plant?"

I shrugged. "Beats me."

"Such a clever plan and it's wasted on you," she teased. "We want to see her reaction to a plant *from Uncle Teddy*. If she thinks he betrayed Clarence, she'll throw it at us."

Clapping my hands, I said "I love it! You're a genius. Did you think about the next step? If she accepts the plant, don't we want to talk to her and find out what she knows?"

Jess gave me a big smile. "Yup. That's where the tea and cookies come in."

"My favorite part of any plan," I said. "I hope she has

107

gingersnaps."

The elevator delivered us to the lobby where we had to dodge between residents to get Marley outside before his bladder burst. Pet therapy was a tough job. Marley deserved a raise.

I thought about what we'd learned upstairs and how it didn't add up. As a family lawyer, I'd never heard of anyone getting a divorce to *save* money. There's an old saying that it's cheaper to keep her and it's true. To put it a different way, love is grand, divorce is twenty grand.

We were halfway to the garden, trying to catch our breath in the stifling heat when Marley stopped in his tracks. He had decided it was time to sniff every blade of grass--a dog's version of reading the newspaper. As we waited, my growling stomach informed me it was lunchtime so loudly that even Jessie heard it. I know because she reached into her pocket and handed me a dog treat as a joke.

I laughed. "I'm not *that* hungry, but I do need to get going. I have a ton of work waiting for me at the office. Text me about Shirley and I'll--"

"There you are! Did you forget to come see me?" Jodi Martin had appeared out of nowhere to confront me about my broken promise.

"Uh, no I didn't," I lied. "I was just on my way, wasn't I, Jess?"

With a toss of her purple tresses, Jessie threw me under the bus. "She forgot."

"It was your fault," I replied. "You kidnapped me."

"Yeah, sure I did," Jessie said with a mischievous smile. "Okay, I'm off to do some pet therapy, catch you later."

I was glad to see the two women interacting as if the Machete Man incident had never happened. When you work in close quarters you need to get along. It also helps if you clean up your mess in the microwave (I'm talking to you, Nelda).

"How was your seminar?" Jodi asked, removing her sunglasses and tucking them into the pocket of her gardening smock.

"Eh," I said. "I don't know what I expected."

Jodi nodded as if you should always expect the unexpected at La Vida Boca. Maybe that could be their new motto. Then Ricky Martin wouldn't have a reason to sue them.

"Let's find somewhere cooler to talk, shall we?"

I followed her back inside where we stood by the glass doors looking out. Everyone else was at lunch so we could speak freely.

"Did you find out anything?" I asked. "Do tell."

She leaned in conspiratorially. "Yes! I grabbed a trashy novel and dropped in on the Book Club. It didn't take long to steer the conversation to the topic of Shirley's outburst but nobody knew what she meant. After a little more prodding, one of the women, Isabel, remembered something. She said that on Memorial Day her grandkids were coming to visit so she went downstairs to the vending machines to buy some snacks. As she made her purchases, she overheard two men arguing in the exercise room on the other side of the wall. She recognized Clarence's voice because of his accent, but she didn't know who the other man was."

"What were they arguing about?" I asked.

"It wasn't clear," Jodi said, "but she heard Clarence say *I know what you did! How could you do that to me? I trusted you.*"

"What did the other man say?"

"He said it was all a mistake and he could clear it up, but Clarence wasn't buying it. He threatened to go to the police and then the man got nasty and told Clarence if he did that, he would go to jail too!"

"What happened next?"

"Clarence said: *You're nothing but a thief, get away from me.* And that was all Isabel heard. She didn't think about it again until the memorial service."

"That's interesting," I said. "I can't imagine what trouble Clarence could have gotten himself into. I didn't think he hung out with anyone here beside the Card Sharks."

Jodi looked thoughtful. "That's true, so we're no closer to knowing who it was."

"Yeah, but you did great! I wish I had some news for you. You got a lot of mileage out of one trashy novel! Can I borrow it, by the way? I need something to read."

With a laugh, she dug it out of her purse and handed it to me. The cover was black and red and the artwork was pretty steamy.

*"The Vampire's Kiss*--are you serious? What's wrong with a good Danielle Steele romance?" The last thing I wanted to do was *feed* my vampire phobia. A sexy vampire was still a vampire.

With a knowing smile, Jodi took the book out of my hand and put it back in her purse. "To each his own," she said, "But you don't know what you're missing!"

"Yeah, I do. Hey, isn't that your botanist friend Eli, alias Machete Man?" I could see through the glass he was lurching towards the doors. "He doesn't look well."

"Oh, my goodness!" Jodi said. "I hope it's not his heart! He has a pacemaker."

She yanked the door open and we ran out. Eli staggered a few more steps before collapsing in a heap on the ground, foam and spittle around his mouth.

"I think he's having a seizure!" I said. "I'll call 911."

As I dialed, Jodi crouched down and tried to help him. "Eli, what happened?"

With eyes half-closed, he struggled to speak and finally managed to utter in a raspy voice "I'm afraid...someone...is trying...to kill me!"

# Chapter Thirty-Four

Jodi gasped. "I can't believe it! Why would anyone want to kill you, Eli?"

I could think of a few reasons starting with the fact that he was a major jerk, but I kept quiet. I don't kick a man when he's down, or literally on the ground, like this guy. I follow my moral compass even when it points me somewhere I don't want to go.

After calling 911 and stating the nature of my emergency, I didn't know what else to do. Eli looked pale but stable and wasn't actively foaming at the mouth, thankfully. Jodi was kneeling beside him in the grass, concerned hand on his shoulder, head tilted so he could whisper in her ear. She nodded that she understood and turned to me.

"Jamie, will you do something for Eli?"

I hate open-ended questions like that. How did I know what I was agreeing to? What if he wanted mouth-to-mouth resuscitation or one of my kidneys? Like any decent lawyer, I preferred to read the fine print before entering into a contract.

"What is it?" I asked, leaving myself a way out.

"Would you run over to the greenhouse and grab his wallet? It's in the top drawer on the right. He needs his health insurance card for the hospital."

"Sure, I'll be back in a flash."

I trekked to the greenhouse stepping carefully in a pointless attempt to keep my shoes clean. To me, Eli's calm request for his wallet seemed out of sync with his wild allegation that his life was in danger but maybe that's how he dealt with stress, by focusing on little details. The important question was why did he think someone was after him? Was he paranoid? Delusional? Maybe he had a crush on Jodi and was desperate for her attention. I hadn't met a single person at La Vida Boca who struck me as a possible killer--except for Eli, of course. Seriously, who would be foolish enough to threaten a man who carried a knife and a machete? Despite having a pacemaker, Eli could almost certainly outrun or outfight anyone there. He was the youngest resident by at least ten years and, in some cases, twenty or thirty.

As I opened the greenhouse door, I braced myself for the tsunami of hot air about to envelop me but still wasn't ready for it. With all the haste I could muster, I grabbed the slick leather wallet from the drawer and reversed course, swimming through air thick as molasses. Exiting the greenhouse I rushed back to Jodi and Eli, resisting the urge to look inside the wallet. I could've justified it by saying I needed to make sure it was his, but I had scruples. Anyway, it was just your basic leather wallet. There was nothing remarkable about it except for a small square of blue paper sticking out of the top with the words *fast relief* on the edge. It looked like a familiar over-the-counter medicine but I couldn't place it.

While I was gone, a small crowd had gathered around the prostrate man, including two EMTs administering aid. As Herb had pointed out the day I met him, ambulances made regular appearances at La Vida Boca. If hunky paramedics were part of the package, my new job did have some perks. It's not always about the money, you know.

"I hope he'll be okay," Jodi said after the ambulance had whisked Eli away. "The paramedic said his vital signs were good. I'll call the hospital later to check on him."

"I'm sure he'll be fine," I said as we walked back inside. "Boy, there's never a dull moment around here, huh? Do you really think someone's trying to *kill* Eli?"

Jodi mulled it over, a tiny crease in her forehead telegraphing her concern. "No," she finally said. "No way. I think he has an overactive imagination."

"Or he's trying to impress a certain someone…"

"Like who?" she asked.

I pointed to her and she laughed heartily. "Oh, yes, men are always pulling stupid stunts to get my attention. I secretly brew love potions with herbs from the garden."

"Nice," I said. "I'm sure there's a market for that. You could start small, maybe open an Etsy store."

Her eyes twinkled. "That will be my next career. Right now, I have my hands full with this one, don't you think? Thanks for your help with Eli, by the way. That was scary! I'm glad you were there."

I nodded. "Happy to help. Now, I have to go take care of my own emergencies which are much less exciting."

On my way out I spotted Wilma in the lobby. With a fake smile, she said to send her an invoice and that she'd see me in a month. Glenda the receptionist even waved good-bye to me. It was official, I was in, I was living La Vida Boca, sort of. Who would have thought? While it gave me a break from divorce work, I'd have to manage my time better and not get mired in the intrigue of assisted living. Putting those words together sounded hilarious, I couldn't wait to tell Grace.

Trekking through the parking lot, eyes glued to my phone, I walked smack into a man doing the same thing and made him drop his briefcase. How embarrassing!

"So sorry!" I said to the well-dressed extremely blond man with the youthful face. "I'm terrible at multi-tasking. I can't walk and chew gum either. Are you okay?"

He laughed as he brushed off his briefcase. "Totally my fault. I'm just glad I didn't walk into traffic. Although I did walk into a parked car once."

I checked out the briefcase, the bespoke suit, the easy-going personality and I thought *salesman.* Pharmaceutical rep or insurance agent was my best guess. I smiled and was turning to go when he asked a question.

"Excuse me, do you work here?"

I shook my head and then reconsidered. "I guess I do, sort of. Thank-you for not asking if I lived here, that would have ruined my day."

He laughed. "That's a good line, I might borrow it. No, I'm looking for someone who does live here and I don't know what he looks like. I was wondering if you could help me out."

I could feel beads of sweat trickling down my neck and I was dying to get going for so many reasons, but my mom had taught me not to be rude. "Not likely since I only know a few residents. Good luck, though."

I was already walking away when he said "His name is Herb Lowenthal and I'm kind of nervous about meeting him, so any advice would be welcome."

113

I came back for that, of course. "Did you say Herb Lowenthal? I do know someone by that name, but I doubt that's who you mean. Maybe it's someone with a similar name?"

The stranger gave me a charming smile and said, "I knew you could help me! It's fate that we collided. Look, we even have matching briefcases." He held his up for me to see.

"Yeah, yeah, next you'll be telling me we have compatible Zodiac signs. What do you want with Herb?" I knew Herb could take care of himself, but I was feeling a bit protective, especially since he'd told me about losing his daughter.

"I understand your reluctance," he said. "Let's start over." He held out his hand for me to shake, so I did. "My name is Bob Beckman, it's nice to meet you...?"

"Jamie Quinn."

"May I call you Jamie?" He smiled sincerely.

"Sure, fine. What brings you to La Vida Boca, Bob? I hope you're not trying to sell Herb something because, if you are, I might feel compelled to give him a heads up." I shifted my weight and put my hand on my hip to show I meant it. Body language makes your point even when your words say something different.

"You are good at reading people and I'm not just saying that. I AM trying to sell Herb something." His pale eyes beseeched me. "I need to make this deal, it's the biggest one of my life. I'm trying to land a contract with his company. Can you help me?"

I was really confused. "How big is big?"

"It's worth a million dollars."

# Chapter Thirty-Five

"You almost had me going!" I said, scanning the parking lot for his cohorts. "What are you doing, a reboot of Candid Camera? I promise to be a good sport, but I'm not very photogenic, I'm afraid."

Bob's expression went from baffled to wary as he realized he'd approached the wrong stranger, that this one wasn't quite right in the head. I was so excited about being on TV that it took me a minute to notice his confusion.

"I'm sorry, but what are you talking about?" he asked.

"What are *you* talking about?" I replied.

"Look," he said, shielding his eyes from the sun. "I thought you could help me, but just forget it, I'll wing it."

He started to walk away and I called him back.

"Wait, Bob, I can help you. What do you want to know about Herb?"

Skeptical, he took two steps towards me. "Why do you want to help me now?"

"I figure we can help each other. I know Herb on a personal level and you know what he does for a living. I'm curious, that's all." When he hesitated, I said, "It's okay, I'll just Google him."

"Alright," he said, closing the gap between us and placing his briefcase on the ground next to mine. "But I can't tell you anything about the deal, it's confidential."

"Fine," I said with a wave of my hand. "What *can* you tell me?"

He smiled. "You, first."

"Herb Lowenthal is a smartass."

"Herb Lowenthal is a genius," Bob said with almost religious fervor.

"He doesn't tolerate fools," I said, remembering how he'd chastised Tillie.

"He holds dozens of patents."

"He doesn't like kiss-ups, so you might have a problem," I teased.

"He's practically a recluse."

"He likes dogs," I said.

"What kind of dogs?" Bob asked.

I shook my head. "You're breaking the rules. Besides, I don't know."

"Fine. He's a pioneer in the medical field."

"He doesn't like personal questions," I said.

"He's not in it for the money," Bob said admiringly.

"He loves fruit," I said.

It was Bob's turn to shake his head. "That doesn't count. Who doesn't love fruit?"

I leaned against a nearby car. "It counts. Now you know what kind of gift to get him. Your turn, by the way."

"He prefers to work remotely."

"That would explain why he's always here," I said. "He can hold a grudge," I added, remembering the story about his daughter.

"Hardly anyone knows what he looks like," Bob whispered, as if there were spies watching us.

"Well, I know what he looks like," I bragged. "That makes me special, huh?" I laughed. "Actually, everyone here knows what he looks like, so what's the big deal?"

Bob stared at me intensely. "They may know what he looks like, but they don't know who he is."

None of this made any sense to me, but it was fascinating nonetheless. "I'll tell you what he looks like if you answer one more question," I said.

"If I can," he said, "I will."

"If Herb is such a recluse, so secretive, so uninterested in money, how in the world did you convince him to meet with you?"

Bob was visibly perspiring now, droplets of sweat on his upper lip. "I didn't. He doesn't know I'm coming."

# Chapter Thirty-Six

"I don't like your chances," I said, after I'd stopped laughing. "Not with a basket of fruit in one hand and a basket of puppies in the other."

"I do have one secret weapon," Bob said, a devilish glint in his eyes. "I'll just say I'm a friend of Jamie Quinn's, that should get me in. Thanks for your help, it was *really* great to meet you!"

"You can't do that!" I yelled as he headed towards the front door. "He'll know you're lying," I bluffed.

Bob waved and smiled and kept on walking, so I let him go. Assuming he made it past Glenda, he wouldn't get anywhere with Herb, who could sense B.S. a mile away. Besides, he still didn't know what Herb looked like.

As I drove to my office, I thought about the enigma that was Herb. If he was such a genius inventor, why did he live at La Vida Boca? I imagined a scenario where he had an ailing wife who needed assistance he couldn't provide and, after she passed away, he stayed on. Or maybe he had a health issue himself and needed assistance. Or maybe he was just hiding from people like Bob. In any case, he must have liked living there or he would have left. Nobody could push Herb around--as Bob would soon find out.

I connected my Bluetooth to the radio for my daily probate lesson, determined to expand my horizons and leave family law behind. (A girl can dream, can't she?) I learned that, while clear communication is critical in any legal document, in probate cases, the communicator is dead and therefore his fuzzy intentions must be interpreted by a judge. Although nobody writes a confusing will on purpose, not knowing when you'll die or what you'll own at the time makes it tricky. For example, what if you decide to leave your blue Chevy to your dear friend Jimbo, but when you die you own a green Ford? Does Jimbo get it anyway? What if you decide to leave your house to your sister, but when you die you have no house. Does she get nothing? What happens if you leave part of your estate to someone who predeceases you? To me, probate law could be

117

reduced to four words--who gets the stuff? Divorce law is also about who gets the stuff--AND who gets the kids, who spent all the money, who pays for what, who is behaving badly, and who gets the family pets for Thanksgiving. By comparison, probate seemed like a walk in the park.

I spent the rest of the day taking care of clients, filing pleadings, and scheduling hearings. Other than one quick call to Petersen's Antiques to make an appointment with the art appraiser, I was focused like a laser. It wasn't until the end of the day when I tried to open my briefcase that I discovered it was locked. That's because it wasn't my briefcase. As if I didn't have enough to do, now I had to track down that annoying salesman or whatever he was, Bob Beckman. To hell with it, if he wanted his briefcase, he could come and get it, I wasn't hard to find. Although I hated to admit it, I was curious about the contents. Bob's boast of a million-dollar-deal had piqued my interest and with the proof so close at hand I was eager to see it. Unfortunately, a three digit lock has a thousand possible combinations and I didn't have that kind of time. Not that I would break into someone else's briefcase, especially when I had a better option. If Bob wanted his case back he'd have to give me some information. I thought it was a fair trade, the deal of the century in fact, and I wasn't budging. It's called leverage, which was my favorite 'L' word, right after 'lottery-winner' and 'ladies drink free'. 'L' was also for losers weepers.

Next item on my to-do list was to check in on Grace. I took out my phone to call, but decided to text in case she was sleeping.

*Yoo-hoo, Gracie, you awake? Feel better? Need anything?*

It took a minute before she replied. *"Ugh! I feel like I was run over by a bus, but thanks for asking.*

*My sick friend! What can I do for you?*

*Can you write an appellate brief about sovereign immunity in a wrongful death action?*

*Sure*, I said, *if you want to lose the case.*

*Never mind, my paralegal will file for an extension. Nick is bringing me soup in a little while, isn't he sweet?*

*He has his moments*, I conceded. *I hate to bug you when you're sick, but any word on my dad's visa?*

118

*Sorry, Jamie, my friend at the State Department is on vacation in Europe, but I left a message. I'm sure I'll hear from him soon.*

*Gracie, you're the best! You get some rest now, okay?*

She replied with zzzzz...

It was frustrating to think about my dad's situation, so I refrained and moved on to my final action item--call Duke. Everyone else in the office had gone home already so I walked into the conference room for a change of scenery.

"Duke's massage parlor," he answered in a husky voice. "Walk-ins welcome."

I laughed. "Is that your new career?"

"I thought I'd try it out, you know, with a select clientele." He chuckled at his own cleverness.

"No sumo wrestlers, then?"

"Hell, no! Don't go spoiling my fun, Ms. Esquire. What's up?"

I grabbed some M & M's from the bowl on the table and crunched a brown one between my teeth. "Just confirming our appointment with the appraiser tomorrow at ten, did you get the painting from Jeff?"

"I did, indeed. It's a strange picture, isn't it? I prefer the ones with pretty ladies, scantily clad."

"There's a shocker," I said. "How about I pick you up at nine-thirty at your place. Or will you still be partying at The Big Easy?" I was joking although it wasn't outside the realm of possibility.

"A man's got to sleep sometime. See you at my place bright and early. Coffee?"

"Don't go to any trouble," I said.

"Wasn't planning on it. What I meant was I like my coffee black with four sugars and I'll need a large. I'm not what you'd call a morning person."

"I'd like to call you something and it's not morning person," I laughed.

"You sound stressed, Darlin'. Remember, walk-ins are always welcome at Duke's massage parlor. Twenty-four hours a day."

119

# Chapter Thirty-Seven

On my way to Duke's the next morning, I decided to make a quick stop at my office to pick up a file I needed. As I parked my Mini Cooper in its assigned space, I saw someone waiting for me. He was seated on the stoop by the back entrance, blond hair almost white in the morning sun and he did not look happy. Just for fun, I took my time getting out of the car.

Once we were face to face, I offered him my friendliest smile. "Bob Beckman, isn't it?'"

He scowled. "You know who I am *and* you know why I'm here."

"Do I? Did you need my help with something?"

"What I need is my briefcase," he snapped.

"What makes you think I have it?" I asked innocently.

"Because I have yours," he said, holding it up to show me. "Your business card is inside, along with some shriveled up grapes."

"Oh, right," I said. "I guess you didn't get far with Herb."

"How do you know that?"

"You'd have been here sooner," I laughed. "You would have opened your briefcase to show Herb what's inside and realized it wasn't yours--unless the case is just a prop. But if it were, you wouldn't be so anxious to get it back. So, you must have struck out with Herb."

Bob shook his head. "No, I didn't. I never even saw him. The woman at the front desk told me nobody by that name lives there."

*Go, Glenda!*

"Aw," I said. "Sounds like a rough day."

"Yeah, whatever. Can I get my briefcase back?"

Nodding serenely, I motioned for him to follow me inside. We walked through the empty waiting room and I led him down the hall to my office.

"I think I've earned a peek inside that case," I said. "We can call it a finder's fee, a reward--"

"What if we call it blackmail?" he interjected.

120

"Gosh," I said, "That's harsh. If you hurt my feelings, I might just forget where I put your briefcase. I'm very sensitive."

The wall of resistance crumbled and Bob laughed. "Sure, fine, why not? And here's *your* briefcase as a show of good faith. I hope you aren't planning to eat those nasty grapes. If you are, please don't do it in front of me." He made a retching noise and I giggled. I could see how he might be fun at a party.

"Do we have a deal?" I extended my right hand.

He shook it. "Deal."

I reached under my desk and slid his briefcase across the carpet. He picked it up, dialed in the combination and two clicks later, the mysterious case was open. I peered inside.

"It's empty!" I said.

Bob shook his head. "No, it's not. Look again."

The second time I looked I saw a black flash drive taped to the black wall of the case.

"That's it?" I was disappointed. He was like a magician in a silk cape who had produced a tattered, fake rabbit.

"Afraid so," he said, closing the case. "It's been interesting, but I'll be on my way now."

He was halfway out the door when I said "Wait--"

"Yes?"

"Can you tell me a little bit about your proposal for Herb? Not the confidential stuff, just why you want to see him."

"Why do you care?" Bob asked, surprised. "You don't seem like a corporate spy."

"I don't know," I said honestly. "I like to connect people, I like puzzles, I'm curious as hell…"

"Three interesting reasons," he smiled and put the briefcase down. "It also sounds like one of those NY Times obituaries."Ms. Quinn liked to connect people, she liked puzzles, and she was curious as hell."

"And she loved ice cream," I added. "Mint chip, especially. Obit done!" I made a check mark in the air. "What's yours say?"

He looked thoughtful for a moment. "Mr. Beckman was a genius and everyone loved him."

I clapped my hands. "Excellent! So, what does Mr. Genius

121

want to say to Herb Lowenthal?"

"He wants to say Mr. Lowenthal, you're the reason I became an engineer. I've studied all your designs and products. You solve problems so elegantly, but I'm afraid I found a mistake in one of your designs, a mistake that could kill people. I also know how to fix it."

"Whoa!" I backed into a chair and sat down. "Are you for real?"

He nodded.

"Then I will get you in to see Herb. Right away!"

# Chapter Thirty-Eight

"You will?" Bob asked. "You'll introduce me to Herb Lowenthal?" He shook his head in amazement. "What are the chances that I'd bump into the right person at just the right time?"

"And steal her briefcase," I added.

"Yeah, it was those delectable grapes--who could resist?" he joked. Glancing at his fancy watch, he said "Do you want to go over there now?"

"I can't," I said, remembering that Duke was waiting. "I have an appointment, but I can go in the afternoon."

We agreed to meet in the parking lot of La Vida Boca at two o'clock. On his way out Bob turned to give me a wink. "Louie," he said, "I think this is the beginning of a beautiful friendship".

"Okay, Bogey," I said, "but I hope this has a better ending than *Casablanca* did."

After Bob left, I felt the weight of responsibility settle on me. Knowing that lives were at stake made me feel like I had to deliver--but what if Herb refused? Herb Lowenthal was a wild card and he wasn't even in the poker club.

After hitting the drive-thru at Dunkin' Donuts on Sheridan Street, I pulled into the multiplex where Duke lived. As usual, broken toys and sports equipment littered the front porch, courtesy of Duke's neighbors. A muscle car on blocks in the side yard had weeds growing around it and a litter of kittens living under it. Someone had left food and water for them and I could see two adorable kittens poking their heads out. I tried to imagine Mr. Paws having to rough it but I couldn't. He was so spoiled that if he had to live under a car he'd insist on a Bentley. I was smitten with the kittens and didn't see Duke until he banged on the passenger window.

I rolled down the window. "Jeez, Duke! What happened to stealthy like a ninja? The door's unlocked, Mr. Private Eye."

He smirked and held up a large rectangular object wrapped in brown paper. "But the back door isn't. I'm not gonna hold this on my lap, now am I, sweet-pea?"

123

"Well, you could if I put you both back there." I said as I opened the lock for him.

With the fake Chagall in the back and Duke in the front, I pulled out of the driveway and pointed my Mini Cooper south towards the city of Dania.

"There's your--" I was going to say "coffee", but Duke was already gulping it down.

He smacked his lips. "Ah, good stuff! You didn't happen to get me one of those pink frosted donuts with sprinkles on it, did ya?"

"Have you met me?" I said and handed him a banana I'd brought from home.

Duke handed it back. "You're no fun."

"Of course I'm fun, I'm the life of the party." I turned right on U.S. 1 and stopped at the red light.

Duke snorted. "Maybe at the old folks' home. I can see it now--you walk in and they yell: Jamie's here, hooray! Bananas for everyone!"

I laughed. "I *am* pretty popular there." Sniffing the air, I said "Someone smells good, like coconut and lime." I turned to take a gander at Duke's ensemble. "Ditched the rapper getup, I see. Two questions--how can you wear alligator boots in this heat and why are you dressed so nice? Hot date later?"

"Nah," he shook his head and his shoulder-length brown hair swayed back and forth. "I dress for success, Ms. Esquire. I fake it til I make it. And who knows when I'll meet a pretty lady? It could happen anytime, anywhere and I gotta be ready."

"There are no smokin' hot babes in the antique store, I'm afraid."

We had arrived and I was circling the block to park behind Petersen's.

He shrugged. "That's okay. The day is young and I'm good-lookin'. Just admit it, Darlin', you think so too."

I flicked him on the shoulder. "At least *you* think so and that's what matters." He laughed. "Before we go in," I said, "I meant to ask if you found out anything else about the painting. Or did you get all those paper cuts for nothing?"

124

Playing dumb, he said, "You mean like something important? Like maybe who sold Earl the painting?"

I gasped. "What? Really?"

"Before I say another word, you have to answer one question," he said.

"Come on! What is it, Duke?"

"Are you gonna do it?"

"Duke, you're a pain."

"Okay, ready?"

"Ask already." I said.

"Who is...the greatest P.I. in Hollywood?"

"How many guesses do I get?"

He looked at his watch. "What a shame! The clock is running out, tick tock."

"Fine. It's you."

"Say it."

"Marmaduke Broussard, III, is the greatest P.I. in Hollywood. Happy now?"

"Oh, yeah. Especially since I recorded you."

# Chapter Thirty-Nine

"*Obviously* I think you're the best P.I., Duke," I said. "Why else would I keep you around?"

"Because I'm arm candy?" He picked up the banana he'd rejected earlier and began wolfing it down.

"Right now you look like a monkey in the zoo, but let's go with arm candy."

He nodded appreciatively with a mouth full of banana.

"Now tell me who sold Earl that painting. Dazzle me with your brilliance!" I nudged him with my elbow, easy to do in a snug Mini Cooper.

Duke looked sheepish. "It's not as exciting as it sounds. I found a bill of sale at the bottom of a box."

"And?" I said.

"Earl bought the painting from a company called *THS Investment Group*. I checked it out on the Florida corporation website and it went inactive years ago."

"Maybe you missed something." I said, pulling my phone out of my purse. I navigated to the Sunbiz website that Duke had already visited. "That's odd, there are no officers or directors listed and the company was only active for a year. Hang on, there's an agent for service of process and it's a law firm. Did you try to contact them?"

Duke laughed, showing off his perfect teeth. "Nah, 'course not! You know you're the only lawyer I talk to. Besides, that's got to be the deadest dead end I've ever seen. That company was dissolved before you were a gleam in your daddy's eye."

"We'll see," I said.

I hunched over my phone and pulled up the Florida Bar website. I knew something Duke didn't--that law firm was still in existence. It didn't mean they'd have useful information, but at least I could check. I called and left a message for the office manager, always the best person to ask about an old file.

I turned off the car. "Ready?"

"I was born ready, Darlin'."

126

We stepped out of the car and Duke collected the painting from the back seat. At the entrance to Petersen's, Duke tried to hold the door for me, but couldn't manage it with his hands full. It was fun to watch him try and I appreciated the chivalrous gesture. I finally had to hold the door open for him and the bell jingled our arrival. Once again, the familiar aroma of one of my favorite childhood memories filled my nostrils. I needed to visit more often, maybe work there part-time. I could organize the bell collection.

The store had just opened and the fleur-de-lis on the window shone on the clean glass. We were the only customers and seemed to be the only people on the premises. I stored my sunglasses in my purse and Duke set the painting on the floor next to the counter.

"It smells like my Grandma Delia's attic," Duke said, rubbing his nose.

"Isn't it great?" I inhaled deeply.

Duke looked at me funny. "If you say so. I prefer the smell of The Big Easy, myself. It smells like home." He crinkled his eyes, amused.

I laughed. "Sure, if your house smells like old beer, cigarettes, and crushed dreams."

Our scintillating conversation was interrupted by someone coming through a door at the back of the store. It was Clarence Jr. and he was perusing some papers in his hand. He looked up, surprised to see us.

"Hello, folks, I'm sorry I didn't hear the bell. Welcome to Petersen's Antiques. Can I help you find something?" He gave us a smile.

"Hi," I said. "We had an appointment with your appraiser at ten."

"Right," he said. "I'm sorry, but our appraiser is out ill. I can help you though, I'm a certified appraiser. What did you want appraised?" He noticed the wrapped package on the floor. "Oh, I see it now, you brought a painting." He took his half-moon glasses out of his pocket. "Let's take a look."

Duke hoisted the painting onto the counter and meticulously peeled back the brown paper. This was a side of Duke

I hadn't seen, his usual approach was more bull-in-a-china-shop. Slowly, the fake Chagall revealed itself in all its glory and it was gorgeous, despite its lack of authenticity--which reminded me of something.

"Did you bring the certificate of authenticity?" I asked Duke.

"You didn't ask me to," he chided, "but I brought it anyway. That's why I'm the best P.I. in town. But you already knew that." When he snickered, I accidentally stepped on his foot.

"Ow!" he said, "watch the boots, girl."

"Did you say you're a P.I.?" Clarence asked.

"Sure am," Duke puffed up with pride.

"Some people need to get over themselves," I observed. "Once he gets started, the humble-brags can go on forever."

Clarence laughed. "What did you bring me today?" He put on gloves and, peering through a loupe, examined the painting carefully for quite a while. He even sniffed it. "It's a beauty," he said. "Looks like Chagall...but it isn't."

Duke piped in, "We already know it's a fake."

Clarence laid down the loupe and looked up at us. "That's where you're mistaken."

# Chapter Forty

Duke was surprised. "Whoa! Do you mean it's, like, the real McCoy?"

I shook my head. "Not possible."

Clarence Jr. cleared his throat politely. "I'm sorry if I gave you false hope, but this is definitely not a Chagall and it's not a fake either. It's a forgery, and that's an important distinction. Fakes are works by artists that are passed off as works by a more important artist. They can also be copies of a work from the same time period, which makes them difficult to identify. In the past, it was normal for the owner of a fine painting to commission an artist to make copies of a piece of art for them. But forgeries are what we call art crime—bogus works by modern-day artists made to look like the real thing." He held the painting at arm's length to take it all in. "It's such a shame…"

He continued to examine the painting, but I wanted him to finish his thought.

"What's a shame?" I asked.

Clarence seemed not to have heard me as he continued scrutinizing the canvas.

"Did I hear you correctly, that you have a certificate of authenticity for this piece?"

Duke nodded. "Sure do." He pulled an envelope from his back pocket and handed it to Clarence.

I gave Duke a look. "Don't tell me you were sitting on that certificate all the way here."

"Hey," he said, with a lopsided grin, "At least I brought it."

Clarence put his loupe back to his eye to read the certificate. When he was done, he returned the document to its envelope. "Just as I thought," he said. "I wanted to make sure I was right." He turned the painting around on the counter so that we could see it. "Do you see the swirling brushstroke in this corner?"

Duke and I both nodded.

"I have a better idea," Clarence said, "I'll show you what I mean."

He walked into the back room and returned with a large book of the coffee-table variety. It took him a minute to find what he was looking for, but then he laid the open book on the counter next to the painting.

"This is a picture of the real painting, *La Nappe Mauve.* Now, can you see the differences?"

"The red is a shade off," I said, "and the horse is a little different."

Clarence nodded approvingly.

"I don't see it," Duke said, disappointed.

"I recognized the style," Clarence said, "although it's been years since I've seen one of his pieces."

We immediately reacted to the news.

"You know about this artist?" I said.

"Who painted it?" Duke asked.

Clarence folded his hands on the counter, like a professor about to enlighten his students. "It was the certificate of authenticity that clinched it, although I knew who it had to be. Many years ago, these forgeries started popping up, mostly Chagall but also a few other artists and they all had a certificate of authenticity that was genuine. It turned out someone was buying original paintings, having a copy made and then selling the forged painting along with the certificate. Eventually, the buyer would sell the original painting *without* the certificate, which wasn't a problem for him since any expert could see it was the real thing. This was before the internet, so it was difficult to track the sale of art. Now, it would be impossible to get away with this scheme."

I bit my lip impatiently. "Who sold the original?"

Clarence shook his head. "They never caught the person."

"What about the painter?" Duke asked.

"Ah, he disappeared years ago, but we know his name. He was trained in Europe and called himself Andre."

"That wasn't his real name?" I asked.

"Probably not," Clarence replied. "It was such a shame."

"What was?" Duke asked.

"Andre was enormously talented. It was a loss for the art world that he didn't use his talent to produce original work. Who

130

knows what he could have produced?"

Clarence picked up the painting again and turned it over to look at the back. He picked up the loupe from the counter and examined the frame. Suddenly, a look of alarm crossed his face and he turned pale. At that moment a few customers walked in and Clarence hastily handed the painting to Duke.

"Thanks for coming in, folks. I have some things I need to take care of now. Good luck." He started to walk away.

"Wait," I said, "don't we owe you any money?"

"Don't worry about it," He said before disappearing into the back room once more.

"What the hell just happened?" Duke asked.

"I have no idea," I said.

# Chapter Forty-One

"Do you mind if I hang onto the painting for a few days?" I said.

Duke and I were driving back from the antique store discussing what we'd learned which admittedly wasn't much.

"Sure," Duke said. "I know you like it and Jeff can't stand having it around. It just reminds him of his lost inheritance."

"Thanks."

I *did* like the painting, but that wasn't why I'd asked for it. I wanted to study it, figure out why Clarence Jr. had been so unnerved. I do love a good puzzle.

As I negotiated my way down U.S. 1 in heavy mid-day traffic, I found it hard to believe that it was still off-season. Once the tourists arrived in November, cars with license plates from all fifty states and every Canadian territory would take over the road. Counting them was an irritating way to pass the time, but those of us with a touch of OCD couldn't help ourselves.

"Well," Duke said, scratching his chin, "that was a fun outing but I can't say it got us anywhere. We know the forger's name--which may not be his real name---but we have no idea who pulled off the scam. Maybe Andre did that too, but so what?"

"I think it was a good lead. There's some follow-up I can do--internet research, talk to a few art experts--"

"Hey! Where are you going?' Duke interjected.

"Isn't that your house? Would you rather be dropped off somewhere else?"

"Aren't you gonna buy me a drink after all that hard work I did?"

I laughed. "It's the middle of the day, buddy! Some of us have a job."

"Fine. How about lunch--with a few drinks to wash it down?"

I shook my head regretfully. "I'd love to, but I have another appointment. Rain check?"

"I'll hold you to it." He grinned at me. "Don't make me wait too long, or you'll be buying me Dom Perignon."

"You'll get a two-for-one happy hour, my friend. Just like always."

"Deal," he said.

I pulled into his driveway for the second time that day and he hopped out of the car. "Don't you go having fun without me, Ms. Esquire."

"Pinky swear!" I said.

I left Duke and headed to La Vida Boca, my new home away from home. It took me a solid forty-five minutes to get from Hollywood to Boca but I was still early for my appointment. After I parked, I sat in my air-conditioned car reading e-mail and catching up on the news. I had become a news junkie recently and needed a fix every few hours--as if the world wouldn't survive if I didn't keep up. I remembered my mom watching CNN constantly, but I was much worse. I was engrossed in a story about a window washer miraculously surviving a forty-five story fall when the phone in my hand rang and caught me by surprise. The number looked vaguely familiar.

"Hello, this is Jamie Quinn."

"Hi, this is Patty Ryan returning your call. I'm the office manager at Lewis & Lewis."

"Oh, right!" I said, "That was fast. Thanks for returning my call. I have a crazy question for you. Your firm represented a company about forty years ago--"

"--Did you say *forty years ago?*"

I laughed. "Yup, that's right. Anyway, there's a painting involved that may or may not be a forgery and I was hoping you could give me some information. I know it's unlikely, but I'm following every lead."

"Wish I could help, but we're only required to keep files seven years. Our policy is to keep them for ten, but then we shred them."

"That's what I thought you'd say. Too bad. In this case, your firm was the designated agent for service of process for a corporation."

"Oh, you should've told me that in the first place," Patty

133

said. "We keep that information in our database forever. Even years after a corporation is dissolved, it can still be sued. What's the name of the company?"

I sucked in my breath. "That's great news! The company was called *THS Investment Group*."

"If you'll hold on, I'll look it up."

Three minutes passed, but it seemed like much longer. Finally, Patty came back on the line.

"You're in luck."

"How so?" I asked.

"One of the managing members of that corporation is still a client, after all these years."

My pulse kicked up a notch. "Can you put me in touch with him? Or her?"

"I'm afraid I can't do that--client confidentiality."

"Wait," I said. "Could you ask them to contact me?"

"That, I can do."

"Fantastic!" I gave her my number and thanked her profusely.

I was feeling good when I got out of the car because I had a lead! It wasn't even my case, it was Duke's, but I was still excited. As I started to walk across the parking lot, I remembered the parcel in my back seat and turned around. I didn't want anyone stealing the fake Chagall thinking it was valuable. After carefully stowing the picture in my trunk and making sure nothing could damage it, I walked into La Vida Boca.

The lobby was filled with the usual crowd. I looked around for Bob, but he wasn't there yet. Among the sea of white hair, one head stood out because it was dyed purple. I strolled over to the sofa where Jessie was sitting with her uncle.

"Do you live here now, or what?" I greeted her. "Where's your trusty sidekick?"

Jessie giggled. "I don't live here--yet. I just stopped by to bring Uncle Teddy his medicine. Marley couldn't come because they won't let him into CVS."

"That's a dumb rule. Corporate headquarters will be hearing from me," I joked.

"Thanks! What are you doing here?" Jess asked.

"I'm meeting someone."

Jessie jumped up from the sofa. "Will you excuse us a minute, Uncle Teddy?" She grabbed me by the arm and pulled me out of earshot. "I have to tell you something! I went to see Shirley Petersen."

"Without me? What happened to us bringing her a plant and then eating all her cookies?"

"Yeah, well, I saw her walking into her apartment and decided to talk to her. I gave her my condolences and said my Uncle Teddy was devastated to lose his friend, Clarence. She was gracious and thanked me, so I knew she didn't blame Uncle Teddy. Then she invited me in and we had a chat. She's something else!"

"How so?" I asked.

Jessie looked amused. "Let's just say her conversation was peppered with salty answers."

"What does that mean?"

"She swore like a sailor!" Jess laughed her musical laugh. "I guess she needed someone to talk to because she told me about how they were planning to get divorced."

I gave Jessie a stern look.

"I swear I didn't ask! She said they were doing it to protect their assets, but she didn't know why Clarence wanted to put everything in her name. She didn't want a divorce, but he insisted it was necessary."

"Did she say what started all this?"

"She wasn't sure, but sometime in May Clarence was looking at the auction websites like he always did and became very upset by something he saw there. She asked him what was wrong, but he refused to talk about it. After that, he became depressed, angry and worried. She didn't know what to do to help him."

"That's so sad," I said. "Does she know who betrayed him?"

"Clarence told her someone *had* betrayed him, but wouldn't tell her who it was."

"Did she say anything else?"

"There was one more thing. She said she'll never forget

how Clarence looked when he collapsed on the shuffleboard court, that it was awful."

"Why, what happened?"

Jessie's eyes grew wide. "She said he was foaming at the mouth like a rabid dog."

# Chapter Forty-Two

"Oh my God!" I said, and that's when it dawned on me. "Hang on a second, did you hear about Eli?"

"What's Eli got to do with anything?" Jessie scowled at the mention of her nemesis.

"He collapsed outside yesterday and was taken to the hospital. He was foaming at the mouth too! There's something going on around here..."

"What should we do?" Jessie asked, alarmed.

"It's too late to find out what killed Clarence, but we can still find out what happened to Eli. I don't know if he was released from the hospital yet, have you seen him?"

"No, but I didn't look for him either."

"Okay," I said. "Jodi is friends with him, she'll know where he is. After my appointment, I'll track her down."

We started walking towards her uncle, who was on his cell phone.

"Will you let me know what you find out?" Jess asked.

"Definitely."

Teddy had stopped talking and was now dialing a number. A ringing sound came from my purse and I pulled out my cell.

"Hello, hello? Is anyone there?" I said.

"Jamie, is that you?"

"Of course it is--" I stopped mid-sentence. I was now face-to-face with Uncle Teddy, who was also talking to me on the phone. I laughed. "Why are you calling me? I'm right here."

But he wasn't laughing. In fact, he didn't look well at all.

"What's wrong, Uncle Teddy?" Jessie asked.

He didn't say anything, apparently too upset to speak. I sat down next to him and put my hand on his arm. Jessie sat down on the other side.

"Are you okay?" I asked gently.

He nodded.

"Do you want to tell me why you were calling me?" I used my soothing voice, the one reserved for distressed clients.

He nodded again. "My lawyer's office just called."

I stared at him. It was my turn to be speechless.

Jessie looked at the two of us. "Can someone please tell me what this is about?"

"I'm not sure yet," I said to her. Speaking to Teddy, I said "Is your attorney Lewis & Lewis?"

"Yes."

"Are you, I mean, were you involved with a company called *THS Investment Group*?"

"Yes, I...I was," he stammered.

"Who else was part of that company?" I asked.

"It was me and my buddies, the poker club. T-H-S stood for Teddy, Harry--"

"And Stanley," I said, finishing the trio. "You were an investment group, what did you invest in?"

"Just one thing--a painting. Clarence convinced us to buy it. He said we could resell it and make a lot of money."

"And you did."

He nodded.

"Was this the painting?" I found the photo on my phone I had taken of the fake Chagall.

The elderly man made a choking sound, but soon recovered. Jessie ran off to find him a glass of water.

"My lawyer said you were calling about a forged painting," he whispered. "Was that a forgery?"

It was my turn to nod.

"Damn it, Clarence!" he croaked.

"Do you think Clarence knew it was a forgery?" I asked.

"Absolutely not!" Teddy defended his friend. "But I think he found out. That would explain his behavior these past few months, why he was afraid to tell us what was bothering him."

And why he wanted to protect his assets through a divorce, I thought. He was afraid of getting caught. Now, the argument he had with that mystery man made sense. That man was involved too.

"Teddy," I said, "did Clarence have any enemies?"

"No way, everyone loved him."

"Did he tell you about an argument he had with someone

138

here?"

"No, and I can't imagine Clarence arguing with anyone," he said. "Do you know what happened to that forged painting?"

"I do. My client's father bought it. He thought he was leaving his children well-off when he died."

Teddy covered his face with his hands. "I'm so sorry, I had no idea." He looked up at me. "Will we go to jail for this?"

"Definitely not," I assured him. "You didn't know."

Jessie returned with a glass of water in her hand and a blond man in tow.

"This guy was looking for you," she said.

Unaware of the drama unfolding on our sofa, Bob Beckman looked very happy to be there. He grabbed Teddy's right hand and shook it with enthusiasm

"It's such an honor to meet you, Mr. Lowenthal."

# Chapter Forty-Three

"Right church, wrong pew, young fella," Teddy said, back to his old self.

"Pardon me?" Bob Beckman looked mighty confused.

"He's not Herb Lowenthal," I explained. "If you'll excuse us," I said to Teddy and Jess, "we have to go find Herb."

I turned to go, but Teddy tapped me on the arm. "I want to make this right," he said.

"We'll talk some more," I promised.

"Make what right?" I heard Jessie ask as I led Bob away.

"I'm not off to a great start, am I?" he said as we approached the reception area.

I glanced over at him, taking in his shoes buffed to a high sheen and his suit with its coordinating tie. He didn't have a hair out of place; I wished I could say the same.

"You forgot the basket of fruit and the basket of puppies," I said.

"Meaning?"

"You might've overdone it a tad. Herb is a no-frills kind of guy. Think Warren Buffet, plainspoken, no nonsense, but with bushier eyebrows. Don't worry, it will be fine. I'm just messin' with you."

We were standing in front of the reception desk and, for once, Glenda wasn't on the phone. It was nothing short of a miracle.

"Hey Glenda, I was looking for Herb, do you know where he is?"

"I believe he's in the library," she said primly.

Bob couldn't let it pass. "Don't you remember me? I was in yesterday and I asked for Herb Lowenthal. You told me there was nobody here by that name."

She gave me a ghost of a smile. "I must not have heard you correctly."

Bob was muttering under his breath, so I said "Yeah, speak up, Bob. You should learn to enunciate."

It would be embarrassing to say I got lost trying to find the

140

library, so I won't say it. In my defense, I'd only seen it once and La Vida Boca's winding corridors all looked the same. After the third wrong turn, Bob noticed we were going in circles.

"Do we need a GPS?" he asked mildly.

"I knew I should've left a trail of breadcrumbs the last time," I said.

Just then, Sylvia the card dealer from the poker club walked by and steered us in the right direction. I had zigged when I should have zagged--the story of my life.

"I hope he's still here," Bob said once we reached the door.

"Aw, come on. It didn't take us *that* long to find it," I said. "I'll go in first, wait here."

I cracked the door open and peeked inside. Herb was there alright and he was alone, typing away on his laptop. He hadn't noticed me yet. Now that I knew he was a genius inventor and successful businessman, I saw him in a different light. I tried to reevaluate our prior conversations, but still couldn't wrap my head around it. He was just Herb to me. His wanting to hire me though, that took on a whole new meaning. As much as I wanted a career shift, I hated being in over my head where I could screw things up in an epic way. I already had enough trouble sleeping at night. If Kip were here, he'd say: *You can do it, Babe,* but I knew better. I'd known me longer.

"Knock, knock," I said. "I hope I'm not bothering you."

Herb stopped typing and motioned me closer. "You, bother me? Not possible, Jamie Quinn. Is it time for another seminar already?" He chuckled. "Or are you here to borrow a book? I recommend *If Life is a Bowl of Cherries, What Am I Doing in the Pits?*"

I laughed. "I've actually read that one. I'm here to ask for a favor."

"For you? Anything." He smiled broadly.

I was glad to catch him in a good mood although I wasn't sure where to start. How do you tell someone they may have designed a product that could kill people? That's hard to sugarcoat. I'd leave it up to Bob, but first I had to convince Herb to talk to him.

"Well, I, um, want to introduce you to someone who's a big

141

fan of your work."

Herb's expression changed immediately, going from surprised to annoyed. "I live here to keep people from bothering me, Jamie Quinn. I'm not mad at you because you didn't know that, but please don't waste my time." Then he resumed typing, his face a closed off mask.

"Herb," I pleaded, "can you spare just a minute? This man has something to tell you, it's really important."

With flared nostrils and angry eyebrows, Herb snapped back "And I care about this, why?"

"Because people might die!"

# Chapter Forty-Four

"People, which people?' Herb asked testily.

Frustrated, I said, "I don't know their *names*, Herb, does it matter who? If they die, it will be your fault, isn't that enough?"

"My fault?' Herb gave me a piercing look. "What's with the melodrama? So, spit it out already, Jamie Quinn."

I crossed the room and sat down at the table across from him. "We haven't known each other very long, but I can tell that you're an honorable man with a good heart. You must care about people or you wouldn't make medical devices that save lives."

Herb relaxed. "You don't really know me. I'm not as honorable as you think, but if you want to put me on a pedestal, who am I to say no?" He smiled warmly. "What do you want me to do?"

I sighed with relief. "There's a man outside who says he found a mistake in one of your devices that could be fatal. Will you talk to him?"

"For you, I'll do it. Send him in, but tell him my bite is worse than my bark." He laughed at his own joke.

I reached across the table and patted his hand. "Thanks, Herb! I knew you would do the right thing."

I walked into the hallway where Bob was waiting. "You're up," I said, "But tread lightly."

Bob reacted as if I'd told him he won the lottery--not the jackpot, but enough to buy some happiness. "Fantastic! You're awesome, I won't forget this."

"Don't worry, I won't let you. Now, break a leg." I gave him a little shove into the room. "Herb, this is Bob. You boys get to know each other." I blew them a kiss and shut the door.

What a day I was having, I was exhausted from doing nothing. I wanted a break from divorce work, but this wasn't what I'd had in mind. They say be careful what you wish for--or at least be very specific. I wasn't ready to talk to Teddy again, or answer Jessie's questions, so I wanted to avoid the lobby but I needed somewhere to chill out. I knew just the place. I headed to the garden where I sat on a bench in the shade where I could watch birds and squirrels and contemplate life. The toasty bench and chirping birds were so soporific that I soon dozed off. The next thing I knew someone was saying my name.

"Hey, Jamie, are you awake?"

"Five more minutes, Mom…I'm not ready to get up," I groaned.

The sound of quiet laughter made me open my eyes and close my mouth. I was grateful no bugs had flown into my gaping maw while I was asleep.

"That's sweet, but I'm not your mom." Jodi Martin was sitting next to me on the bench, hair tucked under a floppy hat, gardening gloves poking out of her pockets.

"Sorry about that, how long have you been here?"

"Just a few minutes. You looked so peaceful; I wanted to let you rest a bit."

"Then why did you wake me up?" I laughed.

"Because lunch is over and the residents will be out soon. I didn't think you'd want them to see you passed out on the bench."

"Very thoughtful," I said, stretching. I rubbed the sleep from my eyes. "There was something I was supposed to ask you, but my mind is blank. Oh yeah, did Eli come back from the hospital? Do you know what was wrong with him?"

"I haven't seen him, but I talked to him yesterday and he sounded good. When I called the hospital they said they had no record of him but then I called his cell and got him. He said he was in the emergency room and that's why they couldn't find him. They planned to keep him overnight, but he was fine."

"What about his story that someone tried to kill him?" I asked.

Jodi's brow furrowed. "He didn't mention it. Maybe he was overwrought at the time."

"There's a reason I'm asking. Remember how he was frothing at the mouth? I just found out Clarence was too, right before he died. Do you think something around here is poisoning people, like bug spray or a chemical?"

Jodi blanched at my question.

144

"What's wrong?" I asked, alarmed.

"It's probably nothing..."

"But?"

"Remember that plant I showed you, the White Baneberry?"

"I'm not sure I do," I said.

"It's also called a Doll's Eye," she clarified.

"Of course! How could I forget a creepy plant like that," I said. "Why?"

"All the eyes are missing, someone stripped them off. I just noticed it this morning."

I wasn't getting her point. "What's the significance?"

"I researched the plant and it's quite poisonous--the berries are dangerous. They can induce what looks like a cardiac arrest and..."

"And?" I asked.

"Frothing of the mouth."

# Chapter Forty-Five

I jumped up. "What? We need to call the police! Even if Eli accidentally poisoned himself with the plant, Clarence sure didn't. And who took all the berries? What are they planning to do with them?" I started pacing in front of the bench, something I do when I'm nervous.

Jodi shook her head. "I think you're overreacting, Jamie. When my father died of a heart attack, he also foamed at the mouth. There might be no connection between Clarence and Eli. Are you familiar with Occam's Razor?"

"Sure," I said. "The simplest solution is usually correct." I took a deep breath. "So, you think Clarence died of natural causes and Eli accidentally poisoned himself?"

She nodded.

"Okay, then who took the berries?"

She frowned again. "Someone who didn't know they were poisonous? Someone who wanted them for decoration?"

"Maybe..." I wasn't convinced, but still willing to consider her theory.

"I tell you what," she said, standing up. "Let's go inside and see if we can find out who took the berries. If we have to search every apartment, we can have the staff do it. Is that a good plan?"

"It's a start," I said.

We made our way out of the garden, wending around the stone path before exiting through the gate. We passed the volleyball area, the tennis court and the shuffleboard court and were walking towards the pool when we heard a piercing scream coming from that direction. We broke into a sprint and arrived just as a crowd began to gather at the deep end. Jodi pushed her way through and stopped at the edge, shock registering on her face. There was a body in the pool, a tall black man with salt and pepper hair. I recognized him right away--Stanley from the Card Sharks.

"Call 911!" I yelled at the closest blue-haired senior citizen. "We need to get him out of the pool!"

Somebody had already alerted the staff and two burly male

146

aides were charging through the glass doors. Without hesitation they jumped into the pool fully clothed and turned Stanley over so his face was out of the water. Then they pushed and pulled him over to the stairs at the shallow end and propped his head and shoulders on the top step to begin CPR. I was impressed with the staff's lightning-fast reaction in an emergency. No wonder this was a five-star facility.

I was so distraught my hands were shaking. Jodi was a wreck too.

"This is awful! Did Stanley usually swim at lunchtime?" I asked. "He's wearing his bathing suit, so it's not like he fell in."

Jodi nodded. "Yes, he did like to swim--especially in the summer."

We watched the ongoing rescue attempt. From the looks of it, there wasn't much hope. Jodi's face was ashy and I thought she was going to be ill.

"I know everyone here is old," I said in a quiet voice, "but Stanley is the second person from the poker club to die in the past two weeks. I don't think it's a coincidence."

Jodi couldn't handle it a second more and ran to the bushes where she threw up. When she returned a few minutes later, she looked fragile, as if she would break in two.

"I don't believe it," she said in a whisper.

"Believe what?" I asked.

"That someone is murdering the residents. I've been here for five years and I've seen this pattern before--several deaths in a short period of time. It's not that unusual. Many of our residents have beaten the actuarial odds, you know? They outlive their peers, their spouses, they win the longevity game, but eventually their time comes too. That's life, Jamie, it's precious and unpredictable."

I started sniffling, overcome with emotion. I couldn't work at a place where I made friends with the residents only to watch them drop dead one by one. It was too much for me. "I have to go, I'm sorry."

Jodi gave me a hug, which I sorely needed, and I left. I took the long way to the parking lot, walking around the perimeter of the building so I wouldn't have to see anyone. I reached my car and was about to make my escape when someone came up behind me and tapped me on the shoulder.

"So close," I said under my breath.

"We have to stop meeting like this," he said with a laugh.

Turning around, I tried to manage a smile. "Yeah, why *are* you always lurking in the parking lot, Bob?"

"I could ask you the same thing," he replied. "Hey, are you okay? You look like you lost your best friend."

I shook my head. "Just got some bad news, but I'll be okay, thanks. You, on the other hand, look like you just found your best friend. Together, we could pose for the Greek comedy and tragedy masks. How did it go with Herb?"

Bob did a little jig. "It couldn't have gone better! Thanks so much for making that happen."

I leaned against my car. "When does the life-saving begin? Aren't lives at stake as we speak?"

"Kind of," he hedged. "I'll start out as a consultant and if that works out Herb will make the position permanent."

"Doesn't he have to recall the defective devices?" I was worrying about strangers now, in case I didn't have enough on my plate.

"Jamie, I suspect you're not a techie. What the device needs is a software patch that can be downloaded from the website. It actually works fine, but it can be hacked into remotely. That's why it's so dangerous."

"Then I'm very glad I could help," I said, and I meant it.

"It was fate that you stole my briefcase." He laughed.

"That you stole mine is what you meant to say," I teased.

"Precisely!" Bob handed me his business card and gave me a peck on the cheek.

"Here's how to reach me," he said. "Call me if you need anything, I owe you big time." He gave a slight bow. "Here's lookin' at you, kid!"

As he walked away, I said, "You know, Turner Classic Movies isn't the only channel on TV. Pictures are in color now!"

He laughed and waved good-bye.

It was time for me to head home where I planned to eat

Chinese take-out straight from the container and soak in the tub until my fingers pruned. I might even have a glass of wine or three while I was at it. Who says I don't know how to have a good time?

# Chapter Forty-Six

The next morning, my cat alarm clock woke me up way too early. The emotional turmoil from the day before (along with a significant amount of wine) had lulled me into a good night's rest and I wanted to sleep in but *someone* didn't get the memo. Mr. Paws (who has a mean streak) decided to start *his* day by jumping on my pillow, sitting on my head and swishing his tail into my nose and mouth. If I didn't get up soon, I'd be coughing up a hair ball.

Grudgingly, I rolled out of bed. "You can be replaced by a dog. Just remember that." He flicked his tail at me and sniffed but I think he got the message.

For once, I didn't check my phone first--it was a bad habit anyway. Instead, I had a leisurely breakfast on my patio where I made the decision to work from home, maybe take my laptop to a coffee shop like all the hip millennials did. Thank-you, modern technology!

As fond as I was of the residents of La Vida Boca, I didn't know if I could keep working there. Although I'd seen my share of death over the past couple of years, those people hadn't been my friends, I didn't even know them. Working at La Vida Boca raised the stakes too much for me.

Ready to tackle some work, I threw on a pair of jeans and a t-shirt and went outside to grab the file I'd left in my trunk. It was a contentious case that required several motions plus a memorandum of law, enough to keep me typing all day. When I opened my trunk I encountered a large wrapped object I'd forgotten was there--the fake Chagall. Oops, I mean the *forged* Chagall. I carried the painting into the house and laid it on the sofa where I removed the paper and flipped it over. What was it Clarence Jr. had found so upsetting? I went into my bedroom and fetched a magnifying glass my mother had bought to read fine print. I examined every inch of the painting but found nothing. I had to stop because my eyes were starting to hurt, so I gave up and went to a coffee shop to work.

With an iced latte sweating in its frosty glass and a table all to myself, I was surprisingly productive, generating pleading after pleading in under two hours. I realized I wasn't as productive at home because I was easily distracted. I could've blamed Mr. Paws (I was still annoyed with him), but it may have had something to do with a fridge full of snacks and a TV stocked with recorded shows. The coffee shop had started to fill up and a young guy with dreadlocks and a political shirt parked himself at the table next to mine. He set up his laptop and then asked me if I would keep an eye on it while he ordered coffee. Of course, I said. I literally kept an eye on his computer, but only because it was interesting. People used to decorate their cars with bumper stickers and now they did the same with their computers. This one had a Jamaican flag, a Salt Life sticker, a peace sign, and a New Orleans Saints logo--clearly, he was a fan. Staring at that last sticker, it dawned on me what Clarence Jr. must have seen on the back of the painting. Suddenly, I couldn't wait to go home and confirm my theory but I had to wait for the guy to come back. He must have had the most complicated coffee order ever, but he finally returned and I took off.

Ten minutes later, I was home wielding the magnifying glass again. Now that I knew what I was looking for, it didn't take me long to find it. On the top left corner of the frame I could just make out a faint gold fleur-de-lis--just like the emblem for the New Orleans Saints--and the logo for Petersen's Antiques. Not only had Clarence Sr. convinced his friends to buy the phony painting, he had sold it to them himself! That would explain why he was so upset, why he thought he would be financially responsible, why he wanted a divorce. It also told me that Clarence Jr. was unaware of what his father had done or he would have recognized the painting *before* he saw the fleur-de-lis. Finally, it told me that the person Clarence had argued with was in on the forgery. Clarence had said *I trusted you.* Maybe the person responsible for an international forgery scam had been at La Vida Boca arguing with Clarence! This was serious, way above my pay grade and certainly above Duke's. I knew who to call although I hated to do it.

I picked up my cell and found his number in my contacts.

He didn't say hello because he had to be a smartass. "Quinn! Are you calling to say good-bye?"

151

"Why would I do that, Nick? I haven't said hello yet."

"Aren't you off to film your new show, *Jamie Quinn, FBI Secret Weapon?*"

"It's in the works," I said. "Don't worry, I'm still casting you as the villain."

"I wasn't worried," he chuckled. "What can I do for you?"

"Well...I'm not sure where to start. There are four words I really hate to say and I'm having trouble getting them out."

"Let me guess," he said. "*You were right, Nick.* Or is it *I was wrong, Nick.*"

"Neither. It's *I need your advice.*"

"That's not as much fun. Okay, see you here in fifteen," he said and hung up.

*Good-bye to you, too, Nick.*

# Chapter Forty-Seven

One of Nick Dimitropoulos's many annoying qualities was his penchant for punctuality. Normally, I'd have no problem getting to his office in fifteen minutes no matter where I happened to be in Hollywood, but I took the time to change into a more professional outfit. Also, how did he know I was even in Hollywood when I called? I knew I'd be late and that I'd catch hell for it.

Like all the State Attorney's offices in Broward County, Nick's office was inside the courthouse. Although everyone entering the building had to pass through a metal detector and have their bags searched, the State Attorney's office had an extra layer of security. You couldn't go in unless they buzzed you in. Considering they put people in jail for a living, it was understandable.

Thirty minutes after our phone call, I was in Nick's waiting room with its sterile décor and boring reading material. Current issues of the Florida Bar and American Bar Association magazines, as well as a brochure titled *Information for Victims and Witnesses of Crime*, were there to provide hours of rollicking entertainment. When the door to the inner sanctum swung open five minutes after I arrived, I expected an assistant but it was Nick himself and he was giving me the stink eye.

"I did call to say I'd be late," I preempted him. "You shouldn't make such horrible expressions, Nick, your face might freeze like that. Didn't your mother warn you?"

He didn't say a word, just walked back to his office. I could follow him or not, he didn't seem to care. Once he sat down at his desk, I sat in a chair facing him. He pretended to be busy signing documents and wouldn't look at me, so I waited. After a few minutes of giving me the silent treatment, he gave up.

"Quinn, I'm a busy man and I was nice enough to carve out some time for you because you're Grace's friend--"

"--Oh, don't you pull the Grace card on me, Dimitropoulos! You wouldn't even know Grace if I hadn't introduced you. Besides, you owe me so many favors I've lost count. So I'm fifteen minutes late, why are you freaking out?"

He smiled almost imperceptibly. "I am not freaking out. I just have a lot going on and then there's the campaign…" he trailed off.

"There it is," I said. "Who told you to run for office, Mr. State Attorney?"

He laughed. "My mother! Right after she told me not to make faces."

"It all makes sense now," I said. "I'm sorry to take your time, but I do need your advice. Or something."

"Give me a hint, Quinn, work with me a little," Nick said, giving me his full attention.

"Okay, a crime was committed forty years ago and it's just come to light."

Nick's eyebrows were high on his forehead. "Forty? As in Four-O? Have you heard about the statute of limitations? The only crime I could prosecute after four decades is murder." He paused. "Are we talking about a murder?"

I shook my head. "Forgery, well, fraud really."

Nick looked thoughtful, his square jaw turned to the side. "When was this fraud discovered?"

"Maybe last February?" I guessed, knowing that Earl had died in January.

"You might have a case," Nick said. "Fraud can be prosecuted within one year of when it was discovered. Of course, you'd have to find the perpetrator and that's a cold trail to follow."

I nodded, but didn't say anything because I was thinking.

"If that's it then, glad I could help. Next time, save us both some time and start with a Google search," he said, kidding/not kidding.

"What if I told you someone had purchased expensive art pieces, had forgeries made and then sold the forgeries? And what if I told you I knew the store where one of the forgeries was sold? What if I told you I believed the perpetrator was still alive and in South Florida?"

"I'd say, is this a plot for your new series? Seriously, do you have any proof of any of these claims?"

I thought about it. Did I? I had a certificate of authenticity.

I had a frame with a fleur-de-lis on it and I had Clarence Jr. who knew the painting had come through his store when his dad ran it. I had a woman who could testify she heard an incriminating argument between Clarence and an unknown man; I had the partial name of the artist who forged the painting. I had a bill of sale from the Card Sharks to Earl under their defunct corporation and I had an insurance policy for a forged painting.

I shook my head. "Not really."

Nick sighed. "Quinn, what are we going to do about you? What advice did you want me to give you?"

"I'm not sure," I admitted. "It seemed to me like this was kind of a big deal, a string of art forgeries, lots of people being defrauded out of lots of money, the perpetrator still on the loose. I guess I'll tell my client he's out of luck."

"What client?" Nick asked.

"The client whose father was defrauded."

"What did he think he was buying?"

"An original Chagall."

Nick's pen slipped out of his hand onto the desk. "Where is this painting now?"

"In my car."

"In your car? Dammit, Quinn, how do you keep doing this?'"

"Doing what, Nick?"

"You don't even know, unreal! Could you go get the painting now?"

"Sure, Nick." I stood up and walked to the doorway. "I sense you're about to give me that advice I came for."

# Chapter Forty-Eight

"I made a phone call while you were gone," Nick said.

"Glad to hear it," I said. "Anyone I know?"

When he didn't answer I let it slide and laid the painting on his desk. "Here you go, one forged painting, as advertised. Isn't she a beauty?"

In broad daylight, the colors were even more breathtaking and powerful. This piece constituted art, even if it was a copy. Andre, whoever he was, was a genius--as well as a master forger, of course.

"I'm starting to think you really are the FBI's secret weapon," Nick commented as he examined the picture.

"Make fun all you want, but then I'll have to kill off your character in the first episode."

"I'm not joking," he said with a pointed look that took me aback.

Before I could respond, there was a knock on the door.

"Would you let her in, please?" Nick asked, as if I should know who she was.

I stood up. "Man, why are you being so weird? I mean, weirder than usual."

Opening the door, I squealed with delight at seeing my old friend.

"Jayashree Patel!"

"How are you, Jamie?" She gave me a hug. "I always feel the urge to call you *Babe*." She laughed. "I'll try to resist."

Jayashree looked like a Bollywood star with her flawless skin, delicate features, and long, silky black hair straight out of a shampoo commercial; it was hard to believe she was a top FBI agent. We'd met when she led a sting operation at Broward County Parks Department with Kip's help. He was happy to participate although it almost got him killed. We met again when I happened upon a money laundering operation involving a notorious Russian hacker. She thought my name was *Babe* because that's how Kip had me listed as a contact in his phone.

156

"I'm fine, thanks--unless you're about to tell me the Russian mob is after me." I pretended to bite my nails.

With a laugh, she said "Definitely not. Eugeny Belov isn't even in the country. We're close to apprehending him though."

"Whew! That's great news. Why are you here then? Unless you can't tell me because it's classified." I glared at Nick, who refused to tell me anything, classified or otherwise.

"I'm here to see you," she said, surprised I didn't know.

"You're in Hollywood just to see me?" It was my turn to look surprised.

Nick felt the need to jump in. "Quinn, it's always like *Who's on First* with you. Agent Patel is here right now--in this room--to see you. She's in Florida for a case."

Jayashree smiled. "I *am* here for a case and I'm hoping you can help."

"Hear that, Nick?" I smirked. "She needs *my* help."

He sighed. "We follow procedures and you stumble onto evidence and don't even know what you have. There's no justice."

"Aw, don't pout, Nick," I teased. "I'd be happy to give you lessons in The Jamie Quinn Method."

Jayashree laughed. "I still can't tell if you two are friends."

"We're frenemies." I said and Nick nodded in agreement.

"Now I understand," she said. "Is this the painting?" she walked over to Nick's desk. Turning to me, she said, "Do you know how long the FBI has been looking for this?"

I ventured a guess. "Forty years? That's how long my client's father had it."

"Not quite. This is the last piece in an international art scam that the FBI has been working on for twenty years. The man behind this scheme purchased original art and also bought worthless paintings from the same time periods so he could use the frames. He hired a forger to make copies which he then passed off as originals using the certificates of authenticity. Later on, he would sell the originals. He had no problem keeping this scam going until the internet came along and his luck ran out. He tried to sell an original painting through an auction house but the owner of the forgery, a wealthy Japanese businessman, saw it listed online and alerted the FBI. Unfortunately, the scammer slipped away and we've been waiting for him to surface ever since. We know that this is the only original painting he hasn't sold yet."

"Holy smokes!" I said. "What's the guy's name?"

"We're not sure," Jayashree said. "He always uses an alias, but he's Caucasian and he would be in his late sixties or early seventies by now."

"You know this isn't the original," I said. "So, why do you need it?"

Jayashree nodded. "I see why you're confused. The original painting was briefly listed for auction at Sotheby's last May. The auction house informed us immediately but before we could close in the listing was removed. We traced the owner's IP address to Hollywood Florida."

It dawned on me what she was planning to do. "You want to use this painting as bait?"

"Exactly! If the scammer sees it, he'll either buy it or try to discredit it as a forgery. At least, that's what we hope. The fact that he listed it for sale may mean he needs the money."

Nick had been sitting quietly, which was an unusual sight, rarer than a blood moon or an albino tiger. I knew it wouldn't last.

"Quinn, you told me that the scammer is in South Florida. How do you know that?" he asked.

"Ha!" I crowed. "That proves it--you *were* listening to me. I do say important stuff once in a while, don't I?"

"Could you answer the question after you're done taking your victory lap?"

I stuck my tongue out at him. "Fine. It's complicated--"

"Isn't it always?" Nick complained. "You'd make a terrible witness, Quinn."

"Yeah, I know. Okay, here goes. An antiques dealer named Clarence Petersen acquired the forgery forty years ago. He thought it was genuine and convinced some of his friends to buy it as an investment. They bought it and resold it to my client, Earl Rappaport, who held onto it until his death last January. When his children tried to sell it, they discovered it was a forgery. Clarence Petersen must have seen the painting listed at Sotheby's in May because he confronted the person who sold it to him and the man threatened him, saying he was complicit."

Nick's eyes were bugging out of his head. Jayashree clapped her hands with excitement.

"Wonderful!" She said. "Now, where can we find Mr. Petersen?"

# Chapter Forty-Nine

I sighed. "The cemetery. He died at the beginning of July."

"That's disappointing," she replied.

"For sure," I said.

"Hang on a minute, Quinn," Nick said. "Where did you get your information about Clarence Petersen and his conversation with the scammer?"

"You're not going to like it," I said.

"I bet," Nick said. "But go ahead and tell us anyway."

"My client hired Duke Broussard to find out if he had any recourse for his father being scammed. Duke found the bill of sale and then I located the people who bought the painting and sold it to Earl--but I swear they didn't know it was a forgery!"

"Fine, fine," Nick said. "Calm down, I wasn't planning to prosecute them. Get to the part about the conversation."

"Okay, I took a part-time job at the assisted living facility where Clarence lived, but I never met him because he died before I started there. Anyway, I went to Clarence's memorial service--"

"I thought you had never met him?" Jayashree said.

"Right! I thought so too, but it turned out I *did* know him from when I was a child. I didn't know that I knew him when I went to his service, I just wound up there by accident--"

"Of course you did," Nick interjected.

"Go on," Jayashree prompted me.

"At the service, the widow was angry and said someone there had betrayed Clarence, but she wouldn't elaborate. So, the activities director, the pet therapist, and I agreed we would try to find out who she was talking about."

"Are you kidding me with this story?" Nick said. "Is this a Nancy Drew mystery or a plot from Scooby-Doo?"

Ignoring Nick, I continued. "The activities director talked to a woman at the book club who said she had overheard a conversation on Memorial Day between Clarence Petersen and another man. The gist of it was that Clarence was angry and she heard him say *I know what you did! How could you do that to me? I trusted*

160

*you."*

"What did the other man say?" Jayashree asked.

"He said it was just a mistake but Clarence threatened to go to the police and the man got nasty and told Clarence that he would go to jail too."

"Then what?" Nick asked.

"Clarence said: *You're nothing but a thief, get away from me.*"

Nick said "Let me get this straight. This book club woman related the conversation she overheard to the activities director who then related it to you and now you're telling it to us?"

"Correct."

"Hearsay upon hearsay. And did the book club woman see the man Clarence was talking to?" he asked.

"She did not," I said. "She didn't see Clarence either, but she recognized his voice."

"How could she be sure it was him?" Jayashree asked.

"Because Clarence had a Swedish accent, he was the only person it could've been."

Jayashree nodded. "Do you know how Clarence died?"

"He collapsed on the shuffleboard court, they think it was a heart attack," I said.

I could've brought up my theory about why Clarence and Eli had both been foaming at the mouth and how Stanley had drowned just the day before, but I didn't want them to think I'd lost my mind completely.

Jayashree seemed to be thinking. She walked back to the desk to study the painting again, turning it over and then holding it up to change the perspective.

"Is it possible," she said, "that the man who threatened Clarence is a resident at the facility?"

"I guess," I said. "Or he could have just been there to see Clarence that day."

"Don't they have sign-in sheets and cameras?" Nick asked.

"Yes, they have both," I answered. "If this guy isn't a resident, then at least you might have his face on camera."

Jayashree put the painting down and tied her hair back with a hairband. "Or he could be a resident. Have you seen anyone there

161

acting suspicious in any way?"

I shrugged. I used to think Eli was super suspicious, but then he fell ill and he wasn't even on the premises when Stanley drowned.

"Say the man *is* a resident," I said. "Why would he stick around after Clarence died?"

"Why would he be living there at all?" Nick asked. "He's hiding in plain sight. Who's going to look for an international art scammer at an old folks' home?" He looked quite pleased with himself.

Jayashree smiled. "You may be right. Let's say he moved there originally to keep an eye on Clarence or to learn the whereabouts of the forged painting. But then Clarence died so he stayed there to lie low. We need to smoke him out. We need someone on the inside."

They both looked at me expectantly.

"What do you need me to do?" I asked.

Jayashree put her hand on my shoulder. "Have you ever worn a wire before?"

# Chapter Fifty

"Seriously?" I asked. "You want me to wear a wire? Then what, l walk around La Vida Boca asking each old man if he's an international art scammer?"

Nick laughed at that but seemed to agree with me. "Wouldn't it be easier now that you have the painting to list it for sale and find the guy that way?"

Jayashree shook her head. "If he sensed a trap, it might scare him off. He already tried to list the original and got spooked. This is a better plan. If it doesn't work, we can always list the painting."

"I guess that makes sense," I said, "But can you at least narrow it down? Maybe get a list of all the Caucasian male residents in the correct age range?"

"Of course!" said Jayashree. "This will take some planning. How about we meet up again tomorrow afternoon so I can brief you?"

"I'll clear my calendar," I said.

"Nick, I would appreciate your assistance with this. Are you available?"

He chortled. "I wouldn't miss this for the world! You finally get your TV debut, Quinn."

Jayashree looked puzzled and I shook my head. "It's best not to encourage him."

\*\*\*

It's not like they'd sworn me to secrecy, but I knew I shouldn't talk about going undercover for the FBI--although I was *dying* to tell someone. I thought about telling Kip since he was in far-off Australia, but he would worry that it was dangerous. If I told Grace, I knew somehow Nick would find out. Mr. Paws could keep a secret, but what fun was that? I was like King Midas's barber; he had a juicy secret too. He knew the King had donkey ears, but couldn't tell anyone. When it became too much for him he dug a hole and whispered his secret into the ground. He felt much better getting it off his chest, but it didn't work out that great in the end.

I'd left the painting with Jayashree (at her request) and didn't think anything of it, but as I was driving home, Duke called.

"Hey there," I said, "How's the best P.I. in Hollywood?"

Duke laughed. "Don't you mean the best P.I. in South Florida?"

"I'm pretty sure that's a different guy."

"Ow, that hurts, Ms. Esquire. Especially since I tell everyone you're the best attorney in South Florida."

"Liar," I said with a laugh.

Duke laughed too. "Hey, can I stop by and pick up the painting? Jeff wants it back."

"What? But you said I could hold onto it. Why does he want it?"

"No idea," Duke said. "None of my business, Darlin', but I said I'd give it back. Is that a problem?"

"In a word, yes."

"Oh, no," he said. "Did your cat tear it up or something? You spill nachos on it?"

"No, nothing like that."

"Then, what?"

"Duke, I can't give it to you because I don't have it."

"Tell me you're joking."

"Not joking," I said as I turned into my driveway and parked the car.

"Where is it then? Did you leave it at your office? What is going on with you?" Duke sounded more exasperated than I'd ever heard him and I didn't blame him one bit.

"I really shouldn't tell you this…"

"Tell me what?" Duke insisted.

"You can't tell anyone, you promise?"

"You can trust me. Don't you know that by now?"

I was still in my car--as if it were a cone of silence where I could tell government secrets with impunity. It's not like my house was bugged.

"Okay, Duke, the truth is the FBI has it, but I'm sure they'll give it back when they're done with it."

"What in the world does the FBI want with Jeff's painting?"

"I'm not at liberty to say."

"Fine," Duke said frostily. "I'll tell Jeff to call you then."

"You can't do that!"

"I could stall him, I suppose. But only if you tell me what you know."

"Alright, Duke, you win. The FBI wants to use it to smoke out the real painting."

"Whoa! How are they going to do that?"

"They want me to wear a wire and go to the assisted living facility," I said. "They think the art scammer might live there."

"Well, I'll be damned!" Duke gave a low whistle. "Thanks for telling me. Oh, yeah, there's one more thing."

"What's that?"

"I'm going with you."

# Chapter Fifty-One

"That's not an option," I said. "You can't go with me. You're not even supposed to know about it!"

"What if I just happen to be there?" Duke said. "It's a free country. I may want to check out my retirement options."

"I can't stop you, but you'd better not interfere. You know Nick, he'd have you arrested for obstruction of justice without blinking an eye."

"Don't worry about me, I can take care of myself. And I can keep an eye on you too."

I was touched. "That's very sweet, but these guys are like a hundred years old, I think I can take care of myself too."

"I'm sure you can, Darlin'. You keep me posted, okay?"

"I will. Hey Duke, do you know what you get when you play a country song backwards?"

He laughed. "'Course I do! You get your house back, your wife back, your dog back, and your truck back."

"Can't fool you!" I laughed. "Now, go play a country song backwards and see if it works."

"Will do, talk to you real soon."

I was glad that Duke knew but now I had to worry about him ruining the FBI's best shot at nailing the culprit--and that was my job.

After dinner, I tried to watch a movie on my comfy couch, but I couldn't concentrate. It was hard to imagine that the scammer would be *living* at La Vida Boca, which was why in all likelihood this was a wild goose chase. But what if it wasn't? Who could it be? Of the three hundred residents, more than half were women. Of the men, at least half of them were too old, some too ill, but maybe that was a ruse too. What better way to hide than in a wheelchair? I only knew a handful of people there--could it be one of them? Herb Lowenthal was wealthy (according to Bob), was it him? Teddy loved art, could he be pulling the biggest scam of all, pretending to be the victim when he was actually the mastermind? What about Harry, he seemed affable, but wouldn't a conman have to be charming? Two

166

members of the Card Sharks were dead, was that a coincidence, like Jodi thought, or was that another member cleaning house? After all, they had been involved with the fake Chagall from the beginning. Although I prided myself on being able to read people, what if hubris was clouding my judgment?

Too many questions without answers. How had I gone from taking a side job at an assisted living facility to wearing a wire for the FBI? Nobody could accuse me of looking for trouble this time, not even Nick. I realized I was overthinking this. While it would be exciting to catch a thief, the chances of this scheme working were slim and, in the end, Jayashree would have to list the painting with an auction house. That made me feel better. Having an adventure without repercussions could be fun.

I was dozing off when I heard the unmistakable sound of a Skype call coming through my computer. There was only one person that could be--Kip! I ran to catch the call before he hung up and was rewarded with a sight that made my heart skip. Looking tanned and fit, Kip was a vision from another world. His smiling brown eyes lit up when he saw me.

"There you are!" he grinned. "How's my favorite Sheila?"

"Um, excuse me, but aren't I your only Sheila?" I laughed, joyful.

"Well, there is another little Sheila in my life now," he said turning away from the camera to pick something up. He came back up with a sack in his arms and, reaching inside, took out a tiny creature with a pink nose that immediately nuzzled up to his shirt.

"Oh my God, Kip! How adorable!"

"Isn't she though?" He tickled her tummy and she wiggled happily. "This baby wombat lost her mom in a car accident, so we're keeping her here until she can survive on her own."

"She just broke the cute scale," I said. "Does that mean you're staying until she grows up?" I asked a bit nervously.

"No, silly. She's staying, but I'm leaving."

"Going to Guam?" I held my breath.

"Nope, going to see my girl." He flashed his dimples at me.

"We're talking about me, right?" I joked.

"Yeah, she's the one, the only one, built like an Amazon,"

167

he sang.

I cracked up. "Are you calling me a brick house?"

"Do you want to be a brick house?"

"What I want to be is with you! When are you coming home?"

He picked up a piece of paper and held it in front of the camera. It was a trip itinerary showing a flight from Sydney to Fort Lauderdale-Hollywood International Airport arriving August first. Just two weeks away! I leaned in to blow him a big kiss.

"I can't wait to see you! I've missed you so much I might just rip your clothes off in the airport," I said in my best sexy voice.

Kip threw his head back and laughed, scaring the baby wombat. "We would be all over the evening news, Babe, but that works for me."

"Love you, Kip."

"I sure love you, Jamie. See you soon!"

"Not soon enough. Good-night, I mean good morning--"

He smiled at me. "I think you mean *Good day, mate!*"

# Chapter Fifty-Two

My briefing took place in the State Attorney's office at three o'clock the next day. It wasn't what I was expecting, then again, I watch way too much TV. I assumed Jayashree would present me with a detailed floor plan of the facility and a schedule of where to be at what time using military hours, but it wasn't that structured. And she brought snacks. We were in the conference room adjoining Nick's office, seated at a table with a box of gourmet chocolate chip cookies as our centerpiece.

"So, I'm wearing a wire," I said, grabbing a second cookie from the box, "and what are you guys doing? Are you in a panel truck outside?"

Nick snorted. "This isn't an episode of NCIS, Quinn. There's no panel truck."

I was confused. "Will you be listening to me in real time? Or will I be recorded?"

"Both," said Jayashree. "We will be listening remotely. We only bring the panel truck if we believe our informant might be in danger."

I nodded. Nice to know I wouldn't be in danger. "Will I be wearing an earpiece? I'm just asking because I have really small ear canals and ear buds always fall out of my ears."

Nick rolled his eyes and Jayashree made a note on her tablet.

"How is this going to work?" I asked.

Jayashree gave me an encouraging smile. "Here is the plan, Jamie. We already checked the visitor log and the cameras for Memorial Day and there were no male visitors that day in the right age range. Therefore, we can conclude that the suspect either snuck in to speak with Clarence or he lives there. We've narrowed down the field of potential suspects considerably because we know the suspect moved into the facility within the last five years."

"How do you know that?" I stood up to brush cookie crumbs off my lap, much to Nick's dismay. I hoped he'd be the one to do the vacuuming.

169

"Good question," Jayashree said. "We have proof that the suspect was living abroad five years ago. With that piece of information, as well as the gender, race and age range, we were able to reduce the list to five possible suspects."

I kicked my shoes off under the table. "Only five? That's great! I thought the list would be huge. What do I need to do exactly? Is there a script you want me to use?"

Nick perked up. "Yes, we want you to pretend you're writing a human interest article about the residents of La Vida Boca."

I stared blankly at him. "Uh, Nick, as much as you hate to admit it, I'm an attorney, not a journalist. These people know me. I can't pretend I've changed careers. That's just weird."

"But Grace said you used to write articles for magazines," he said.

"Sure I did," I said. "Back when I was an English Lit major."

"What if you were writing an article for a legal journal?" Jayashree asked.

"Maybe I could work with that," I conceded. "Who's on the list?"

I looked at the list Jayashree handed me and my heart sank; I recognized four of the five names. Herb was on there, as was Teddy, his friend Harry, and Luke a/k/a Mr. Casanova from the seminar. The only one I didn't know was a man named Samuel and I fervently hoped it was him. I would talk to him first.

"What questions am I supposed to ask them?" I said.

Nick handed me a sheet of paper titled *Topics for Discussion* with seven topics:

--*Ask how holidays are celebrated at the facility*
--*Were they there for the 4th of July? How about Memorial Day?*
--*Ask about their background, what kind of work did they do?*
--*Ask if they are Florida natives. If not, what made them decide to move here?*
--*Where are they from originally?*
--*What made them choose this facility?*
--*For Teddy and Harry, ask them additional questions about their*

*purchase of the Chagall: When did it occur? How much did they pay for it? How much did they sell it for? How did Clarence convince them to buy it? Did he say where he got the painting?*

"One question, Nick."

"What is it, Quinn?"

"If I'm supposed to be researching an article, why am I asking Harry and Teddy about the painting? That makes no sense."

"I knew you'd say that." Nick replied. "When you finish your other questions, you can tell Teddy you want to talk to him about the painting. He told you he wanted to make things right and now you want to help him do that."

"Fine, that works," I said, "but I can't do that with Harry. What I can do is ask Teddy if he told Harry about the painting being a forgery and, if so, what was his reaction. Depending on his answer, I can go from there."

"Excellent plan." Jayashree said reaching into a small metal box on the table and removing a piece of costume jewelry. It was a stick pin the length of a matchstick.

"That's pretty," I said.

"Glad you like it, this is the recording device you'll be wearing," she said.

"Ha! That's more like it. And Nick said this wasn't like an episode of NCIS. Wrong again, Dimitropoulos."

Nick groaned. "I can't believe you're our best hope, Quinn. Life can be so cruel."

I laughed. "You're welcome to wear the stick pin and give it your best shot."

"And what will you be doing?" he asked.

"I'll sit in the panel truck and play with all the gadgets."

# Chapter Fifty-Three

I was more nervous about spilling coffee on my stick-pin-recording-device than I was about my assignment. After all, I only had to talk to people and talking was what I did for a living. Like they say, talk is cheap until you hire a lawyer.

It was ten in the morning and La Vida Boca was its usual beehive of activity. Not really, everyone was just sitting around the lobby like they always did. Jayashree's last piece of advice to me was to be flexible because it was a fluid situation--like in court, when a star witness changes his story. Flexible was fine, but my plan was still to interview Samuel first. If he was the scammer (and I hoped he was), then I could stop looking. The receptionist desk was the best place to start.

"Good morning, Glenda, how are you today?"

"As well as can be expected," she said without looking up from her crossword puzzle. "What's an eight-letter word for baby buggy?"

"Carriage?"

"That's it." After she finished writing, she made eye contact. "What can I do for you?"

"I'm looking for a resident named Samuel."

Glenda returned to her puzzle. "We don't have anyone named Samuel here."

Nonplussed, I stammered "But Glenda... you can tell me--I work here. Don't you remember me?"

"I know who you are," she said matter-of-factly, "and I'm telling you, nobody named Samuel lives here." Then she dismissed me by answering the phone that had been ringing since I got there.

Glenda had to be mistaken. I would just ask around until I found Samuel. *Be flexible, Jamie.* Who should I ask? Everyone. I started with a sweet-looking grandma on the closest loveseat. I approached her with a warm smile.

"Excuse me, do you know who Samuel is?"

She took my hand. "Samuel? He's my younger brother."

"That's great!" I said. "Do you know where he is now?"

"I imagine he's out back," she said, nodding her head.

"Okay, is he on the shuffleboard court? In the garden? At the pool?"

With a beatific smile, she said "He'd better be feeding those chickens or he's going to get a beating. Mama always says hard heads make soft behinds."

I heard Nick laughing through my earbud. "Good job, Quinn! You're an ace detective."

"Get out of my head, Nick!" I hissed. "Or I swear I'll throw this earbud into the next flower arrangement I see."

"Don't worry about it, Jamie," Jayashree assured me. "You'll find him, keep going."

It was a setback, but I could do this. If I worked my way around the room, surely, somebody would know who Samuel was. I was about to approach another resident, a man in an armchair reading a book, when someone tapped me on the shoulder. It was Jodi Martin, dressed in business attire in lieu of her gardening outfit.

"What a surprise, Jamie! After the other day, I didn't think you'd be back."

I nodded. "Yeah, me either. Stanley...?"

She shook her head. "It's been tough for everyone, he was well-loved."

"I'm so sorry to hear that."

Jodi looked around before whispering in my ear, "We never found those berries, by the way. We looked everywhere."

I gasped. "That's very bad news. Did you tell Wilma?"

Jodi nodded, her face grim.

"What did she do about it?" I asked.

"Basically, nothing. She said she would look into it," Jodi said. "I'm thinking of calling the police."

"What is she talking about, Quinn?" Nick demanded, taking over my right ear.

"Go away!" I said.

"Excuse me?" Jodi said, confusion in her hazel eyes.

"Sorry! I tell you what--I'll speak with Wilma and make sure she does the right thing, ok?"

"Thank-you! I've been so worried about this. You'll let me

173

know?"

"Absolutely," I said.

After she left, I lowered my head so I could yell at my stick pin. "Nick, I swear, you'd better cut it out."

A familiar voice in my other ear said "Why are you talking to your jewelry, Darlin'?"

I jumped. "Man, you shouldn't sneak up on me like that!" I pointed to my pin and then pointed to my ear and said "Shh" very quietly.

Duke nodded and mouthed "okay."

I took out my phone and typed a message "Turn around so your back is to the camera." I showed him and he complied. Then I typed a second message "I can't be seen with you, you're on your own. Thanks for coming though!"

After giving me a two-finger salute, Duke walked off to who knows where to do who knows what. Not my problem. Once more, I started walking toward the bookish man in the armchair but was stopped by none other than Tillie, who had crossed the lobby to see me.

"Hey Tillie," I said.

"Hello! Did you happen to bring any of that delicious fruit today? That was so kind of you and we appreciated it very much and I was hoping--"

"I'm afraid not," I said. "But I'll bring you some fruit next time, okay?"

Dejected, she trudged away. This time, I made it to the armchair and asked the man about Samuel. Not only had he never met a Samuel at La Vida Boca, but none of the other residents in the lobby had either.

I talked to my stick pin again. "Jayashree, I'm striking out here. Are you sure the guy's name is Samuel? Could it be a mistake?"

After she confirmed that Samuel was in fact a resident who currently lived at the facility, I was determined to track him down. Before going outside to ask around I stopped at the vending machines to buy a bottle of water. As I was leaving, I ran into Jessie and Marley in the hallway and the reception she gave me was chilly.

Arms folded across her chest, Jessie stared me down. "I

174

thought we were friends, Jamie."

"Aren't we?" I asked. "What did I do, why are you upset with me?"

"How do you not know?" she blasted me.

"I'm sorry, but I don't."

"Way to go, Quinn," Nick said, hijacking my ear again. "Glad to hear you annoy other people too."

Since I couldn't respond, I slapped my stick pin with the palm of my hand and it felt good.

"Please tell me," I said.

She shook her head in disbelief. "You were there! You were at the pool when Stanley died and you just left. Uncle Teddy had to watch his friend wheeled out on a stretcher. Do you know how devastated he was? And you didn't even come tell me."

I looked at the ground, trying to find the words to express myself. Finally, I said "Yes, I was there and yes, I left. I left because I was so upset I couldn't deal with it. I didn't think I'd ever come back here. It was just too much for me."

I looked at Jessie and she had tears in her eyes. "Now, I understand. I'm sorry I doubted you."

We hugged it out and Marley wedged himself between us, wanting to be included.

"So, why are you here now?" she asked.

"Doing a favor for someone," I said. "Maybe I can stop by the shelter next week and we can have a fun visit for a change."

Jess smiled. "Perfect! I'll get some pizza."

"It's a date!" I said and we went our separate ways.

I'd almost made it outside when I was stopped again, this time by Sylvia, the card dealer.

"I heard you were here," she said, "and I really need to talk to you."

"I'm kind of busy right now, can it wait?"

"It can't. I need legal advice," she said. "It's an emergency."

"What is this about, Sylvia?"

Looking frightened, she closed the gap between us. In a strained voice, she said "I think Stanley was murdered!"

# Chapter Fifty-Four

"But Sylvia," I said gently, "when Stanley drowned, he was alone in the pool. I saw him."

She leaned in again, as if afraid of being overheard. "That's not the whole story. The day after he died, I went to Stanley's apartment to collect a suit for him to be buried in. While I was there, I found a note on the table that said *Enjoy these fresh-baked cookies.*"

"I'm not sure where you're going with this, Sylvia."

"The note was signed by me! I didn't give Stanley cookies, I swear to you. Why would someone do that?"

She was so shaken I had to guide her to a chair and help her sit down.

"It's strange, but it doesn't mean he was murdered," I said.

"There's more. The day Clarence died, we had breakfast together and he said his oatmeal didn't taste right. That it tasted sweet. Clarence never put sugar on his oatmeal."

"Maybe he got the wrong bowl?"

"No, I'm telling you, I think they were both poisoned! I'm not crazy."

I wasn't convinced that cookies and oatmeal added up to murder, but I had to say something to calm her down. Then the answer came to me.

"Sylvia, I have this friend at the State Attorney's office, his name is Nick Dimitropoulos and he can help you with this. I'm sure he'll conduct a full investigation. Let me give you his private cell number. Do you have a pen?"

It was hard to write with Nick yelling in my ear, but somehow I managed.

After Sylvia left, I took out my phone to look up the Doll's Eye plant. Jodi had told me it could cause cardiac arrest and foaming of the mouth, but I wanted to know more. To my horror, I learned that a number of children had been poisoned from eating the berries, which looked like candy and tasted sweet! If Sylvia was right, someone had poisoned Clarence and Stanley with Doll's Eye--but why kill two members of the Card Sharks? If it was the scammer, it made sense that he would want to kill Clarence, who could expose him, but why Stanley? Suddenly, I understood. He wanted to kill off the poker club so he could sell the real Chagall. They were the only people alive who could tie him to the entire scam! Unfortunately, that didn't eliminate Teddy and Harry as suspects, either one could still be the scammer. And how did Eli get poisoned, was it an accident? He had survived when the other men hadn't. I needed to find Samuel, now more than ever. My thoughts were interrupted by Jayashree's voice in my ear.

"Jamie, what's happening there? You haven't found Samuel, but you did promise an elderly woman some fruit, spoke to another woman about missing berries, patched up a friendship, and discussed two possible poisonings with someone named Sylvia."

I explained my theory about the scammer being a murderer and how, if that were true, it didn't eliminate any of the five men on our list. After some discussion, we agreed to stick to the original plan. Having talked to everyone in the lobby, I went outside and made my way to the shuffleboard court where a couple of men I recognized were playing a game. It was Luke and Duke, Mr. Casanova and Mr. Casanova Jr. Somehow, they'd found each other. I needed to speak to Luke, but Duke being there was a complication. So much for him staying out of my way.

"Hello, gentlemen," I said. "Looks like you two have hit it off, birds of a feather."

"Why, hello to you." Duke laid his stick on the ground and closed the distance between us so he could take my hand. Instead of shaking it, he kissed it. "I don't believe we've met. I'm *sure* I'd remember you, Darlin'."

I laughed. "You're pretty memorable, yourself. How are you doing, Luke?"

"Just dandy. Isn't this guy great?" He pointed at his new friend. "He reminds me of my younger days. The ladies loved me back then."

"Sounds like you have a lot in common. I mean, I wouldn't know since I just met you," I said to Duke, snatching my hand back. "Do either of you know a resident named Samuel?"

Luke shook his lion's mane of white hair and Duke

177

shrugged, playing along.

"I hate to interrupt your game, but could I speak with you for a few minutes, Luke? Would you mind?" I asked Duke.

Duke's eyes widened when he realized Luke must be on my list.

"No problem, I have some things to take care of. I'll see you at Happy Hour!" he said to Luke.

"He's terrific!" Luke said after Duke left. "What a fine fellow, he taught me some new jokes too."

"I bet he did," I said. "He seems like a real joker. Why don't we get out of the sun?"

We sat on a bench by the door and I asked Luke the questions on my list, pretending it was for an article. He was quite charming and I enjoyed our chat, but he was not the scammer. It only took one question, what did he do for Memorial Day? He told me his cousin took him to a barbecue on the beach and he was there all day. He even told me his cousin's name and which beach they went to. It couldn't have been Luke arguing with Clarence that day.

I was standing up to go inside when Duke came tearing through the door chasing an older man, a man who seemed focused on reaching me.

Duke grabbed him by the arm. "I asked you *why* you're looking for Jamie Quinn and you didn't give me an answer."

"Why should I? My business is with her."

Duke stood in front of me. "Her business is my business, that's why. Now, who are you? "

The man looked harmless in his ill-fitting clothes and uncombed hair. Even his glasses were on crooked. There was something definitely off about him. I decided to take a chance.

"What is it you want to tell me?" I asked him.

"I have nothing to tell you. I have papers to serve on you," he sniffed indignantly.

Duke and I knew better. "Are you appointed by the Sheriff's office to be a private process server?" I asked.

"No, I'm exempt from that." He pushed his glasses up on his head. "I'm from the family of Wise, sovereign nation."

My mouth fell open. "Are you--did you send me a letter

178

before? *You're Marcus J. Wise!*"

"And you are in violation of my copyright and also in breach of contract. You owe me one and a half million dollars. Plus interest. Since you just violated my copyright again, now you owe me three million dollars. Consider yourself served!" With that, he dropped the papers at my feet and stormed off.

"Well, Ms. Esquire," Duke said, laughing, "now I've seen everything."

Then I heard an angry voice and, just like a horror movie, the call was coming from inside the house.

"Quinn," Nick said in my ear, "what the hell is going on?"

## Chapter Fifty-Five

"Nothing to worry about, Nick," I said. "Everything's under control, ten-four, over and out."

"What is Duke Broussard doing there?" he demanded to know. "This is an FBI operation, Quinn, not a tea party--"

"Oops," I said, pulling the earbud out of my ear and sliding into my pants pocket. "Sorry," I said to my stick pin, "the earbud just fell out. I told you I had small ears."

Duke grinned at me. "You're gonna catch hell for that."

"I think I already did." I laughed. "You get me into more trouble, Broussard."

"Girl, I get you *out* of trouble." He picked up the papers on the ground. "You want these?"

I shook my head. "I have bigger fish to fry. I'm going to track down Herb now. What are you going to do?"

"I'll be securing the perimeter," he joked.

"You do that," I said, "but chances are the bad guy's already here."

I went back inside and headed for the library which I had no trouble finding after wandering in circles with Bob the last time. Herb was in there, alone, typing away on his computer.

Hi Herb!" I said cheerfully.

He didn't look up. "I don't have time today, Jamie Quinn, I'm very busy."

"Oh, sorry," I said. "I just had one question to ask you."

"Then ask it already."

'Were you here on Memorial Day?"

"What kind of cockamamie question is that? Of course I was here, I'm always here," he said. He seemed tense, his typing frenetic.

"Okay," I said. "Maybe we can talk some more later?" When he didn't respond, I said "you must be working on something important."

He stopped typing and gave me a haunted look that caught me completely off guard.

"It's a matter of life or death."

"I'm sorry to bother you." I closed the door, leaving him alone again.

I realized I'd forgotten to ask him if he knew who Samuel was, which might have been a better question. As I walked down the corridor I heard someone walking behind me. I turned around and saw it was Eli. He looked none the worse for wear after his ordeal. He caught up with me.

"I never got to thank you for helping me that day," he said, sounding sincere.

"Oh, you're welcome," I said. "Glad you're alright. Did you find out what it was?"

He shook his head. "All the tests were negative."

"Weird!" I said. I was going to ask him why he thought someone had been trying to kill him, but instead I asked the question of the day.

"Do you happen to know Samuel?"

His dark eyes flashed. Was it anger? Surprise? He recovered quickly.

"Yes, I do, he's a friend of mine. Would you like me to take you to him?"

"That would be great!" I said. "I really appreciate it. I've been trying to track him down all day."

"Come with me," he said. "We can check his apartment."

We took the elevator to the sixth floor, which I knew was independent living. We walked to the end of the corridor and stood in front of the very last door. Eli knocked, but there was no answer.

"Let's leave him a note," Eli suggested. "I know where he keeps his spare key."

"Oh, I don't think we should go in…"

"Just to leave a note," he said. "It's no problem." He reached behind a potted plant and took out a key. He unlocked the door and before I knew what was happening, he grabbed my arm and yanked me inside. Then he reached into his jacket and pulled out his wicked-looking knife.

"If you scream, I will kill you."

I nodded, terrified.

"I heard you were looking for Samuel, asking everyone. Why are you so damn nosy?"

In a whisper I asked my question. "Are you Samuel?"

"Of course I am, you stupid girl. My name is Samuel Elijah Zeiger."

I didn't think there was any hope that he was not going to kill me, so I scanned the room for a weapon, a way to escape, anything. I decided to keep him talking, try to distract him.

"What happened to you that day you collapsed?"

"I know you looked in my wallet, but you didn't figure it out, did you?" He sneered.

"I didn't look in your wallet! There was a blue piece of paper sticking out, that's all I saw."

Then I remembered why that paper looked so familiar. We had gone through boxes of the stuff in college. It was an Alka-Seltzer packet. Eli had stuck a tablet in his mouth to make it foam!

"Why did you do it?" I asked. "Fake an attack."

"You know why I did it," he said, pulling me into the kitchen.

"So nobody would blame you when the others died."

"Very good," he said sarcastically.

In my panic, I'd forgotten I was wired, that Nick and Jayashree could hear everything. Unfortunately, they didn't know how to find me. Even if I could whisper the apartment number to them, there wasn't enough time for them to send someone. At least, they would have the recording as evidence. Time takes on a new quality when you think you're going to die. Every second seems like an hour.

"If you kill me, don't you think you'll get caught? I'm a bit young to have a heart attack from your poison cookies."

He stopped what he was doing. "You're right. That's why you're going to kill yourself by jumping off the balcony. Five stories ought to do it."

"I'm going to jump out of your apartment?" I was stalling. "They'll still blame you."

"No, they won't. This isn't my apartment." He started pushing me towards the balcony.

182

I heard a siren in the distance and prayed it was someone coming for me. Eli opened the door to the balcony and I tried to twist away. He tried to pull me by my hair but he couldn't get a grip. I kicked and punched at him, but he was stronger than I was. I was inches from the guard rail of the balcony when, all of a sudden, Eli grabbed his chest and fell to the floor. He was dead! I started screaming at the top of my lungs just as the door was broken down and a SWAT team burst into the room.

I don't remember much after that. I'm told I went into shock and they took me to the hospital by ambulance. I finally had my own hunky paramedics and I didn't even get to see them. When I woke up at Boca Regional Hospital a few hours later, I had a lot of visitors. Duke was sitting by my bedside, Grace on the other side. Jayashree and Nick were sitting in chairs by the door.

"Jeez," I said when I opened my eyes, "can't a girl get a little shut-eye before she gets debriefed?"

# Chapter Fifty-Six

"No need to debrief," Jayashree said, gently stroking my hair. "We heard everything. You were very brave."

"You're too damn trusting," Duke scolded me. "You could've died!"

"Yeah," I said, "then you couldn't be my arm candy anymore."

He gave me a smile, although I could tell he wanted to lecture me some more.

Nick walked over to put in his two cents. "Good job today, Quinn."

"Thanks, Nick. Are you being nice because Grace is here?" I teased.

Grace was sitting at the foot of my bed and she leaned forward. "He means it, but I'm mad at you. First, you don't tell me what's going on and then you blithely follow a murderer into his lair. You know it was my turn to rescue you and you didn't give me a chance."

I shuddered. "I'm so glad you weren't there, Gracie! I'm sorry, I won't do it again. All I wanted was a little side job to break up the monotony and somehow I ended up here."

Nick laughed. "I've gotta hand it to you, Quinn--you're the only person who could find trouble at an old folks' home!"

"Speaking of finding trouble, how did you find me?"

"Your stick pin had a GPS tracker in it," Nick said. "It looks like you missed a few episodes of NCIS."

The nurse came in to say visiting hours were over and that I needed to rest. She started to shoo everyone out, but I asked Jayashree to stay a minute.

"What's going to happen to the real Chagall?" I asked.

"Well," she said, "normally it would go into evidence, but since the case is now solved and the perpetrator is dead, it will go to its rightful owner."

"And who is that?" I asked.

"The people with the bill of sale and the certificate of

authenticity are the rightful owners," she said, smiling.

"Yippee! Jeff will be so happy," I said. "Can I be the one to tell him?"

"I'd say you earned that right--and then some. I'm so sorry this happened, Jamie. I never imagined you would be in danger."

"It was my own fault," I said. "Duke's right, I'm too trusting. I have one more question for you."

'Sure, what is it?"

"How did Eli die?"

"His pacemaker malfunctioned," Jayashree said. "Fortuitous timing, I'd say."

"No kidding! Wait, are you saying you think it was, like, divine intervention?"

"If there was an intervention," she paused, "it wasn't divine. More of a math problem someone solved."

"I'm not sure what you mean," I said. "

"Your friend, Herb Lowenthal, he's a genius with math problems, isn't he? Perhaps you should ask him. Good-night, Jamie. I'll stop by to see you tomorrow."

After Jayashree left, I took my purse out of the bedside drawer and found a business card I'd stashed in there. I dialed the number on the card using the hospital phone.

"Bob Beckman speaking."

"Hey Bob, it's Jamie Quinn. How's the new job?"

"It's a dream come true and I have you to thank for it."

"I'm glad to hear that because I need to ask you something."

"Of course, anything at all."

"What's the glitch you found in Herb's design?"

"Anything but that!" he said. "You know I can't tell you."

"Tell me."

"But I signed a non-disclosure!"

"Tell me," I insisted.

"It could cause problems for Herb."

"Tell me."

"I'll get fired!"

"Tell me."

"I'll get sued."

"You could get fired, Herb could get in trouble, I could get sued, but Bob, you're forgetting one thing."

"What's that?"

*"It doesn't take much to see that the problems of three little people don't amount to a hill of beans in this crazy world. Someday you'll understand that."*

Bob laughed. "Fine, I'll tell you, but this stays between us, okay?"

"Okay."

"Herb designs software for--"

"Pacemakers," I said.

"How did you know?"

"Just a lucky guess," I said. "Today happens to be my lucky day."

# Chapter Fifty-Seven

"Why did you kill him, Herb? I'm not saying he didn't deserve it--I mean he did poison Clarence and Stanley and try to push me over a balcony."

We were on our second cup of coffee, eating breakfast together at Herb's favorite deli. It had been a week since my wild day at La Vida Boca and I wanted some answers. To my surprise, Herb agreed we needed to talk.

"I'll tell you why I did it, Jamie Quinn, but that's the end of a long story and I should start at the beginning." He took a sip of coffee, his hand a little shaky. "I told you before that I had a beautiful daughter, she was the light of my life and she died far too young. If I could give her my time on this earth, I would, but she's dead and I'm not. She was so gifted at such an early age that my wife and I sent her to Paris to study when she was eighteen. That's where she met Eli. He was twenty-five, a smooth talker, charming, not like the man you met--he was different then. But he was always a manipulator; someone who took advantage of people, used them and discarded them. He got my little girl hooked on drugs so she would depend on him and do what he said. He exploited her talents and made himself rich off them. When she died of an overdose at the age of twenty-one, he fled the country. My wife died soon after of a broken heart and I swore I would find Eli if it took me the rest of my life."

I was shocked by these revelations, but there were still things I didn't understand.

"So, you tracked him down to La Vida Boca?"

"I did."

"How did you find him?" I asked.

"Through his pacemaker," Herb said. "I designed the software for several models and each pacemaker recipient is registered. That way, the doctors can scan an unconscious person for the microchip and know which pacemaker they have."

"What about the flaw that Bob discovered, where someone can hack into the device? You put that there on purpose, didn't you?"

Herb nodded, calmly admitting to his act of premeditated murder.

"Eli had no idea who you were?"

Herb shook his head.

"Were you ever going to tell him?"

My companion looked thoughtful. "I didn't know what I was going to do. I played with so many scenarios in my head. It wasn't until I learned that he had killed Clarence and Stanley that I knew I had to kill him."

"How did you put all that together?" I was stacking the sugar packets on the table until they fell over.

"The same way you did," he laughed. "I paid attention. But I also had an advantage--I knew what he was capable of."

"Isn't it ironic that he pretended someone was trying to kill him, not knowing someone really was?"

"It's no less than he deserved," Herb said bitterly.

I reached over and touched his arm. "You never told me your daughter's name."

"I think you already know it," he said. "Her name was Andrea."

I was floored. "Your daughter was Andre? She forged all of those paintings?"

He nodded, his eyes filled with sadness.

"What a talent she had, I love her version of the Chagall more than I could ever love the original. It gives me such joy to look at it."

"Thank-you for that, it means a lot to me," he replied.

"Don't thank me, Herb, you saved my life." Tears started rolling down my face, I couldn't help it.

Herb handed me a clean napkin and gave me a tender look. "It was a tragedy that I couldn't save my daughter, but now I see why God let me live so long. It was so I could save you, Jamie Quinn."

# Chapter Fifty-Eight

We drove back to La Vida Boca and I walked him in. As we passed the receptionist desk, I said "Look who I found, Glenda," and pointed at Herb.

She almost smiled before she caught herself. "Finders, keepers."

We said good-bye in the lobby and Herb handed me a large, thick envelope.

"What's this?" I asked.

"Why, you writing a book?" he joked. "Make it a mystery and leave my chapter out."

"Never!" I said, grinning.

"Open it later," he said. "You can give me your answer next week."

"You're so mysterious, Herb," I said and gave him a kiss on the cheek.

I was running late for my next appointment and had to hustle to make it to Hollywood on time. Duke was also planning to be there. When I walked in, I saw my client reading magazines in the waiting room.

"Sorry I'm late!"

"No problem, I was early." He gave me a nervous smile. "Duke said you guys had an update for me?"

"We sure do, Jeff," I ushered him into my office.

Ten minutes later, Duke arrived with a shopping bag which he placed carefully on my desk.

"How y'all doing?" he asked ebulliently.

"We're fantastic," I answered.

"We are?" Jeff Rappaport said. "Does this mean you found out who sold my dad the forgery?"

"Yeah, you could say that," Duke replied, taking a seat next to Jeff. "But those guys didn't know it was a forgery either."

"I see." Jeff looked crestfallen, his last hope gone up in smoke.

"They did want you to know they were very sorry," he

189

added.

"Sorry?" Jeff was incredulous.

"Say, Duke," I said, "wasn't there one more thing we needed to tell Jeff?"

"Pretty sure we're forgettin' something." Duke agreed.

"Oh, yeah! I have this letter for you." I handed him an envelope.

"Who is it from?" Jeff asked.

"A friend of mine," I said, "She works for the FBI."

Baffled, Jeff took the envelope and started reading. Duke and I could barely contain ourselves waiting for him to get to the good part. Jeff's face lost all color, then immediately turned crimson.

"Is this true? I don't understand--you found the real Chagall? The FBI says it belongs to us?"

When Duke and I nodded, Jeff gave a loud whoop and leaped out of his chair.

"Oh, Lord, this can't be happening! How is this possible? My sister's gonna flip out! You two, I can't believe you did this for me! How can I thank you? What do I owe you?"

Duke laughed. "He took the news well, don't you think?"

"I'd say so," I agreed.

"This calls for a celebration!" Duke opened the bag on my desk and took out a bottle of champagne and three plastic glasses. He popped open the bubbly and filled the glasses.

"Aren't you a classy guy," I said.

"First class all the way," he agreed, handing us each a glass before raising his.

"To fine art!"

"To fine art!" Jeff toasted. "And to the best day of my life! How did you do it?"

"That's classified, isn't it, Duke?"

"Yup, classified."

"How can I ever thank you?" Jeff asked. "Send me your bill," he said to Duke.

"Got it right here," Duke said with a laugh, pulling the bill from his pocket.

"Jamie, what do I owe you?" Jeff asked.

"Nothing," I said. "You didn't hire me for this. There is one thing you could do for me."

"Name it," he said.

"I would love to have the forged painting," I said.

"Of course you can have it!"

"Excellent!" I said. "That calls for a drink in the middle of the day."

"Or, as I call it, lunch," Duke said.

# Chapter Fifty-Nine

After our impromptu celebration was over and I was alone in my office, I decided to open the envelope Herb had given me. Inside was a fat packet of papers with a letter on top.

*Dear Jamie Quinn,*

*Remember I said I wanted to hire you? Well, here's the job offer. I'm a rich man and I want to honor my daughter's memory with all that money. I also want to do some good in this world--what else is money for, am I right? I've set up a trust, The Andrea Lowenthal Memorial Fund, and I want you to run it. You would be the trustee and you would be paid an annual salary. Here's what you would have to do:*

*--Try to locate any of Andrea's paintings, including the forgeries, that are still out there and buy them; you can hire that detective friend of yours to help you.*

*--Find a gallery or museum in Boca Raton, Florida that will permanently display Andrea's works. I want to be able to visit them.*

*--Start a scholarship program at Florida universities for promising art students;*

*--Provide grants to the universities and their professors for special art projects, at your discretion;*

*--Fund a chair in the art department of one of the universities in Andrea's name;*

*--Any other project you deem worthy, at your discretion.*

*Do an old man a favor and say yes. I can't think of a better person for the job than you. You have heart, you have brains, and most important, you have moxie.*

*Gratefully yours,*

*Herb Lowenthal*

*P.S. Now you can afford to quit your day job.*

Stunned, I tried to comprehend my good fortune--my dream job had just fallen into my lap! Those good vibes I'd sent out into the universe really paid off, and then some. How could life get any better than this?

I texted Herb one word: Yes!

# Chapter Sixty

"Thanks for coming, Jamie. I hate going to the airport by myself at night."

"I know, Grace, me too. Why are your parents coming to town? Any special reason?"

"Yeah, their friends are celebrating their fiftieth anniversary with a big fancy party at The Breakers."

"How nice! And what's Nick up to?"

"Preparing for trial tomorrow," she said, changing lanes into the airport exit. "I bet you're excited Kip's finally coming home."

My face couldn't stop smiling at the mention of Kip. "Only eight more days!"

"How many hours?" Grace teased.

We parked in short term parking and then walked to the terminal. I was dressed better than I would have been because Grace's parents wanted to take us to dinner. We headed to baggage claim since that's where they said to meet them.

Grace kept checking her watch. "They should be here any minute," she said.

"You're pretty excited to see your parents," I said. "That's so nice!"

"Would you mind grabbing a luggage cart?" she asked, pointing to the other side of the baggage area. "They said they had a lot of luggage. I'd do it, but I don't want to miss them."

"Sure." I turned my back and started walking over there. I was about halfway when Grace called out to me.

"Never mind, Jamie."

"Make up your mind, Grace," I said under my breath and turned back.

My eyes fixed on what had to be a mirage. Then I shrieked and started running.

"Kip! You're here!" Then I was in his arms, kissing his face and crying with joy.

"Jamie!" He grabbed me around the waist and pulled me

193

close like he never wanted to let me go. It was heaven.

"You tricked me," I said, laughing like an idiot.

"I can't believe we pulled it off!" Grace said, coming in for the group hug.

We were in our huddle when Kip said "I brought you a present, Babe."

"Is it an adorable wombat baby?"

"Better," he said. "Take a look."

He pointed to the down escalator filled with people coming to baggage claim. Only it wasn't filled with strangers. Duke was there, waving, Aunt Peg and Adam, Nick, Herb, my new friend Jodi, my step-mother Ana Maria, Jessie, and Uncle Teddy were there too.

"Way to throw a party, Grace!" I was euphoric.

The group reached the bottom and then spread out so I could clearly see there was another person in the crowd. Someone I had loved from a distance, since childhood, since before I ever met him. I broke down sobbing.

"Papi, is it really you?"

Tears were flowing freely down his face, the face I knew as well as my own, my Skype twin.

"Mi hija, my precious daughter!"

I was hugging my dad, he was real, and he was here. I thought my heart would break from being so full. He held my face between his hands and kissed my forehead over and over. He smiled.

"Am I too late to teach you how to ride a bike?" he said with a sweet smile.

I laughed. Ana Maria came over and hugged her husband.

"Yes, mi amor," she said. "Too late for that. But we can teach her to Salsa and Merengue." Then the two of them did a few Salsa steps right in the middle of baggage claim.

Everyone clapped and cheered and started talking at once.

"How did you manage this?" I asked Grace.

"With some assistance from my friend, Greg, in the State Department, of course. It helped that you were pretty distracted with other things." She laughed.

I turned to Kip. "So, you're not going to Guam?"

194

"Well," he said, "I'd still like to go--but only if you'll go with me."

I shook my head emphatically, like a toddler who didn't want to take medicine. "I hate mice! I hate small planes!"

"But how do you feel about me?" he asked.

"You? I *love* you," I said and we kissed again.

"Would you think about going?" he asked.

Maybe it was time for an adventure, time to take a chance. I looked over at my dad. How could I leave when he had just gotten here? We had lost too much time already.

Kip seemed to read my mind. "Hey, Guillermo," he yelled to my dad. "Want to go on an adventure with me and Jamie?"

"Of course I do!" he yelled back.

"Then it's settled," Kip said.

Nick walked over to us, his arm around Grace. "Congrats, Quinn, we're happy for you."

"Thanks, Nick." I beamed.

"I have something for you," he said, handing me an envelope.

"What is it?"

"It's a check from the FBI."

"For what?" I asked.

"Your consulting work in solving the forgery crime," he said.

"Ha! I'm an FBI consultant, Nick. I told you so," I gloated.

"That's you," he said, "Star of the new hit series, *Jamie Quinn, FBI Secret Weapon.*"

THE END

195